COUNTING *on* CHRISTMAS

ALSO BY
TRENTON HUGHES

The Christmas Note

COUNTING on CHRISTMAS

TRENTON HUGHES

SWEETWATER
BOOKS

An imprint of Cedar Fort, Inc.
Springville, Utah

© 2018 Trenton Hughes

ISBN 13: 978-1-4621-2196-0

Published by Sweetwater Books, an imprint of Cedar Fort, Inc.
2373 W. 700 S., Springville, UT 84663
Distributed by Cedar Fort, Inc., www.cedarfort.com

LIBRARY OF CONGRESS CATALOGING-IN-PUBLICATION DATA

Names: Hughes, Trenton, 1991- author.
Title: Counting on Christmas / Trenton Hughes.
Description: Springville, Utah : Sweetwater Books, an imprint of Cedar Fort, Inc., [2018]
Identifiers: LCCN 2018015530 (print) | LCCN 2018027731 (ebook) | ISBN 9781462129157 (epub, pdf, mobi) | ISBN 9781462121960 (perfect bound : alk. paper)
Subjects: LCSH: Fathers and daughters--Fiction. | LCGFT: Christmas fiction.
Classification: LCC PS3608.U376 (ebook) | LCC PS3608.U376 C68 2018 (print) | DDC 813/.6--dc22
LC record available at https://lccn.loc.gov/2018015530

Cover design by Markie Riley
Cover design © 2018 Cedar Fort, Inc.
Edited by Jessilyn Peaslee and Deborah Spencer
Typeset by Kaitlin Barwick

Printed in the United States of America

10 9 8 7 6 5 4 3 2 1

Printed on acid-free paper

To my family.

You are my inspiration for this story.

CHAPTER 1

TUESDAY, DECEMBER 1

Tom VanHansen drizzled maple syrup over a warm batch of Bertha's crisp golden-brown waffles. The sweet smells of buttermilk and cinnamon filled his nostrils, just as they had every Tuesday morning for the past forty-six years. He wore the checkered red flannel his wife had given him for Christmas three years prior, and he sat in his usual booth, the one next to the window with a grand view of downtown Glenn Hills, California. Yet Tom already knew that this day would be anything but normal, and that fact had him on edge.

"Save some syrup for me, Turbo," croaked a man with a weathered face and thin gray hair from across the table.

"Like you need any more syrup, Richard. Your picture could be in the encyclopedia under *diabetes*," Tom responded in his gravelly voice as he struggled with his fork to cut into a waffle. "Where're the dang knives?"

"Easy there, Turbo. You'll get your sugar soon enough." Richard slid a knife across the table.

"Hey, you two, do I have to referee every time?" a plump, rosy-cheeked woman with an uncanny resemblance to Mrs. Claus interrupted as she made her way to their table and set down two piping hot mugs of black coffee. "I'm not afraid to separate you grumpy old men," she warned. Bertha, the owner of Bertha's Diner, was known as a Glenn Hills legend for two reasons: her unmatched sarcasm and cooking the best breakfast west of the Mississippi.

"We may be grumpy, but we ain't old," Tom said as he emptied a packet of sugar into his coffee. To Tom, no food or drink was ever good enough until it had been sweetened. Of course, his diabetes probably didn't agree, but who cared about a silly thing like that?

"Yeah, didn't you hear, Bertha? Seventy-two is the new seventy," Richard added, a wrinkled grin stretching across his face.

Bertha let out an exaggerated scoff. "I need a new job," she said, turning to walk back to the kitchen, her wide hips sashaying from side to side.

Richard used both hands to leisurely raise his mug to his lips. "You think she likes me?" he asked.

"An old geezer like you? Nope." Tom shoveled a giant bite of waffle into his mouth.

They ate their breakfasts in silence while simultaneously reading their own copies of the local newspaper, the *Glenn Hills Times*, just as they had every Tuesday morning since Tom and Holly moved in next door to Richard and Marlene back in 1972.

"You see that dumb, liberal mayor wants to put in a new town hall? Can't wait until he shakes us down for more money," Richard said through a sip of his hot coffee. Their mutual political beliefs had been the foundation of their friendship all those years back, but Holly and Marlene had grown annoyed of their husbands' long-winded conversations rather quickly. Eventually they drew up a plan to limit Tom and Richard's political talk to just one morning a week, and thus Tuesday mornings at Bertha's Diner were born.

"The days of smart fiscal spending are long gone. Now it's all about how much money the good-for-nothing government can get out of us working men." Tom hadn't actually worked since retiring as an electrician ten years earlier, but that didn't stop him from still referring to himself as part of the "struggle." He'd come from a long line of blue-collar workers who believed the government had no right to their pocketbooks or bedrooms. It pained him that as he'd aged, he'd succumbed to living off government benefits to get by every month, especially after all the recent medical bills. He wasn't ever going to admit it to Richard though.

Richard set down his newspaper, then looked up at Tom intently. "So what time is she coming today?"

Tom glanced over his newspaper, already frustrated by the question. He knew Richard was referring to his daughter, Noel, whom Tom hadn't seen in two years. In fact, he hadn't even heard from her until he'd gotten the call on his landline a week ago, and he still hadn't come to grips with the fact that she was coming home.

"Sometime tonight," Tom grumbled. He pulled the newspaper back up to signify he was done with the conversation.

"How long is she staying?" Richard pressed.

Tom shrugged and continued reading, even more annoyed. The truth was that he really didn't know how long Noel planned to stay. When he'd received the call, all she'd said was that she and Bryan were splitting up, and she and the kids needed a temporary place to stay. Tom had been hesitant when she didn't offer anything in the way of explanation because of what'd happened the last time they'd spoken, but he'd eventually agreed.

"Have you told her the truth yet? About the accident?" Richard asked.

He just didn't know when to stop. Again, Tom knew exactly what Richard was asking, and again, Tom didn't want to answer. "For your information, Putz, no, I haven't."

Richard shook his head. "You're going to have to tell her at some point."

Tom ignored the comment and then reached for his mug. Suddenly, a hand appeared out of nowhere and slapped something white against the window. Tom jerked back, spilling his coffee all over himself.

Richard's fork clattered to the floor, and his head snapped toward the window.

"Gosh dang it!" Tom yelled, standing to wipe the coffee from his shirt and pants, which were now sticking to his skin.

Outside the window, a young Hispanic teenager watched wide-eyed before jumping over to the door.

"I'm so sorry," the boy pleaded as he ran to grab napkins.

"What in heaven's name are you doing hitting the window like that?" Tom demanded.

"Bertha hired me to paint snowflakes for her Christmas window display," the boy explained through rapid breaths. He held up a paintbrush for proof.

Tom took the napkins and began to rub out the coffee.

Richard took one to wipe away the syrup that had splashed across his face. "Seemed more like Bertha hired you to kill us. I nearly peed my pants," he wheezed.

Bertha burst into laughter from the kitchen. "Sets you two old-timers straight!"

"Sorry, sir," the teen said again.

Tom looked down at the black coffee stain stretching across the hem of his faded red flannel. Holly's favorite shirt of his was now ruined. "Yeah, yeah. Just be more careful next time," he returned grudgingly.

"Will do, sir," the boy said with an apologetic bow.

Richard continued to blot the syrup from his face. "Kids."

The boy waved apologetically once he was back outside. Then he raised the paintbrush to the window. White snowflakes quickly began to take shape.

"Guess it's that time of year again," Richard stated, looking up at Tom with expectant eyes, as though waiting to see how he would react.

"Guess it is," Tom replied curtly.

Christmas had always been Tom and Holly's favorite time of year. It was easy to get lost in the magic of the season living in Glenn Hills, as every year it was home to the famous Christmas Cup Competition. The city council put cups around town, collecting money all season to give as an award to the best-decorated house in the city. Nearly every resident participated in some way, shape, or form. Because of this, Glenn Hills was known as the most festive town in all of California. People came from miles around to check out the immaculate Christmas light displays that could be found on just about any street in the entire city. Tom himself even used to participate, until the accident.

Tom and Richard continued eating their waffles in silence while the boy worked meticulously to paint a winter wonderland right outside their window.

A few minutes later, music blasted from below the table.

Tom jolted upright, his heart jumping to nearly double the speed. "I swear I am going to have a heart attack today," he bellowed while looking down in a frantic search for the source of the commotion.

Richard looked down as well.

Tom reached into his pocket, realizing the music was coming from his cell phone. He hadn't had a call on his cell phone in weeks, if not months, and had completely forgotten the sound it made when it did receive calls. He held it out in front of him while the music continued to play loud for everyone around them to hear. The other patrons looked over with annoyance on their faces.

"Answer it," Richard demanded.

"How do you work this gizmo?" Tom asked, tapping his finger against it to try and stop the commotion, his blood pressure starting to rise. He'd gotten the touchscreen phone a few months back when Richard had vowed that smartphones were the only way to go. The salesman from the store swore it was the easiest thing Tom would ever use. Liars.

"Press the dang button!" Richard yelled.

"There is no button!"

Richard pulled out his glasses to help. "Give it to me." He squinted at the screen as the music continued to chime through the diner. Then the music stopped and a message that Tom could read from his seat was displayed.

One Missed Call.

"Gosh dang it," Tom snapped.

Suddenly, the music started again.

Richard tapped his own fingers against the screen to try to answer it, but the music kept going. Now everyone in the restaurant was watching the two old men.

"Give it back to me," Tom said, hastily grabbing the phone from Richard to resume pressing his own finger against the screen. The music continued. In the background, Bertha howled from uncontrollable laughter. "This stupid thing is broken!" Tom yelled.

"Can I help?" a voice asked from beside him.

Tom looked up to see the young Hispanic boy. He hesitated for a moment but then nodded.

The boy reached over to slide his finger across the screen, and a second later, the music stopped.

"Thank goodness," someone called from a few tables away.

Tom grabbed the phone and held it to his ear. "Speak," he demanded, furious at whoever could possibly be interrupting his Tuesday morning breakfast.

"Hi. It's Noel."

"Noel?"

"Yeah." Her voice was lackluster and quiet. "We're here."

"You're at the house?" Tom asked, flabbergasted. She'd said she'd be there in the evening, so he hadn't cleaned up or even prepared at all yet. How could she be there already? She lived over ten hours away.

"Yeah, we're waiting outside."

"I'll be there in a few minutes," he finally answered. Tom looked down at the phone, but he couldn't figure out how to hang it up. He glanced up at the boy still standing beside him, then handed it to him. The boy pressed the button to end the call.

"Thanks," Tom mumbled, barely loud enough for anyone to hear. The boy simply smiled, then walked away.

Tom stared down at his half-eaten plate of waffles.

"Noel?" Richard asked in surprise, watching him from across the table.

Tom nodded, expressionless.

"Well, then, I better get the check."

Tom flew down the street in his 1995 Ford Bronco at a whopping twenty-two miles an hour. He turned the corner to his street, Hidden Meadows Lane. An orange glow from the morning sun hung above the local mountains.

Glenn Hills was a relatively small residential neighborhood in Northern California known for its strong sense of community, its picture-perfect downtown, and the rolling foothills that surrounded it. The homes were very big in majority, with gorgeous green yards, and safe, neighborly streets. While stringing Christmas lights along his roof, a neighbor waved to Tom. Tom rolled his eyes and continued driving past the massive modernized houses toward the home he and Holly had lived in since 1972.

Built on a corner lot, behind three tall oak trees and a dying brown-grassed lawn, the faded tan house had red eave-linings, mostly infested by termites now, and outdated roof shingles on top. It was the only house on the entire street that hadn't been updated since they'd moved in all those years ago. Even Richard next door had given in like the sucker he was and renovated in the late nineties. Tom spotted an unfamiliar minivan parked in his driveway as he approached.

He swallowed the lump in his throat and pulled in beside the minivan. Inching forward, he could see boxes upon boxes filling the back of the minivan. His breathing began to quicken. He hadn't seen Noel or his grandkids in over two years. Evan was five now, Brittany seven, and Trevor already twelve. Would the kids even remember him? How was he supposed to act? He definitely wasn't a *kids* kind of person.

He parked the Bronco and looked over through the front window of the minivan. Four faces stared back. Another lump caught in his throat. He reached for his door and took his time getting out.

"Grandpa!" yelled a round-faced young girl in overalls. Her blonde pigtails bounced on her shoulders as she ran toward him and then clasped her arms around his waist.

Tom looked down at the unexpected embrace. She had to be a whole foot taller than the last time he'd seen her. He was suddenly struck by how long it'd been. "Hello, Brittany," he said, his voice curt.

After she let go, a short boy with a bowl cut stepped toward him, smiling from ear to ear.

"Hi, Grandpa!" he exclaimed in a soft but excited high-pitched voice. The boy latched onto Tom's waist and squeezed tight.

Again, Tom didn't hug him back, but he couldn't help noticing the way he pronounced his words now, compared to the mumbled toddler talk from the last time he'd seen him. "Hello, Evan," Tom croaked. Then he looked up to another boy, who was now leaning against the front of the minivan.

The skinny boy with spiky golden hair and a black shirt glared at him and then looked away. His jeans were slouched below his hips, with his blue-striped boxers hanging out of the back for anyone to see. He looked far different from the baseball-jersey-wearing, always-smiling grandson he'd been two years ago.

"Hello, Trevor," Tom called.

Trevor ignored him.

"I said 'Hello,' Trevor."

Trevor rolled his eyes.

Tom stared at the child and tilted his head, realizing that his grandson really had changed. "I said—" he started to say again, but then a woman approached from the back of the minivan.

Her flowing, sunshiny hair was shorter than it had been the last time he'd seen her, and her thin heart-shaped face looked slightly more aged. Her hazel eyes were slightly puffy and red, faint signs that she'd been crying. Tom knew she was trying to hide it, never being one to cry in front of others. He couldn't believe she was actually here. He'd gone the last two years thinking he'd never see her again, and yet here she was. She moved toward him, and for a second he thought she was going to hug him. Instead she stopped a few feet away.

"Hi, Tom," she acknowledged.

He lowered his head, looking away. She was still calling him "Tom." Long gone were the days she called him "Dad."

"Noel."

An uncomfortable silence hung in the air for several beats.

"Well, shall we head inside?" she asked, gesturing toward the back gate at the end of the driveway. Yes, the back gate was the quicker way into the house from the driveway on the side of the house, but guests typically opted for the front. With all the time that had gone by, Noel and the kids felt more like guests than family, which left the whole situation feeling strange.

Tom nodded, then opened the gate to a backyard of dying, overgrown grass as he hurried to make his way toward the back door, looking back over his shoulder as he did.

Evan and Brittany smiled as they walked across the yard, taking in the unfamiliar scene.

Noel followed behind them, looking over the barren lawn, while Trevor lingered at the gate.

Tom opened the back door into a dark and dingy living room. The smell of musty old carpets and leftover sausage hung in the air. To the right, an aged burgundy couch, draped with some of his dirty clothes, sat next to a faded green recliner and a carved wooden coffee table. A few soiled dishes from the past week sat atop it. Tom rushed to pick them up.

"Ew! What is that smell?" Brittany squealed.

"Brittany, manners," Noel snapped from outside.

Tom flushed as he picked up his old plates of food. If he'd known they would be here this early, he certainly would have cleaned a bit more. No one besides himself had been inside his house in over two years. He carried the plates to the kitchen, where a few more dishes and old food containers sat in the sink.

"Be respectful," Noel whispered while coming through the door.

Tom pulled out a trash bag and began to toss the paper plates and Styrofoam containers inside. Then he made his way to the table and shoved in some of the papers and piled junk mail that had been sitting on top of it.

"Wow! What is that thing?" Evan yelled in astonishment.

Tom turned his head to see Evan and Brittany mesmerized by his 1982 television. The one-hundred-and-twenty-pound TV with a thirty-inch screen was an absolute classic. Who needed one of those fancy, newfangled flat screens anyway? It was obvious the corporate powers-that-be designed them to break in a ploy to get more money every year or two. He wasn't going to be one of the idiots to fall for that scam.

"It's a TV," Noel said. "I see you kept the house the same, Tom," she called from the living room.

"Huh? Uh, yeah," Tom grumbled while tying off the trash bag.

He moved toward the couch and grabbed his pile of dirty laundry from it. Then he hauled the pile through the living room toward his bedroom. The wood boards of the hallway creaked as he hustled across them.

He opened the door to his bedroom, revealing an unmade bed and two shirts on the floor. He picked them up and tossed all of the clothes into the hamper. Then he reached across the bed and smoothed out the wrinkles in the purple duvet—Holly's choice, of course.

The full-length mirror caught Tom's attention when he glanced up. Thinking about it, Tom couldn't remember the last time he'd stopped to look at it. He stared, taken aback by the sight of himself. The man reflected back at him was almost unrecognizable, with unkempt gray-ing hair, a coffee-stained flannel, faded jeans, and beat-up old boots. His unshaven beard was overly bushy and his weathered and wrinkled face held an almost permanent frown. Tom lifted his hand to his head and used his calloused fingers to comb his hair to the side before finally looking away.

He took off his ruined flannel, which left him with a hollow pit in his stomach as he looked at it. "Stupid kid," he grunted to himself. He replaced it with a brown one.

When he looked back at the mirror, he tried to raise his lips to form a smile. It looked forced, but then again he hadn't had reason to smile in over two years. He buttoned the last button and turned back to the hallway.

In the living room, Evan and Brittany sat together on the recliner. Trevor stayed outside. Tom could see him through the window, staring into the bushes. The sink was running in the background, and after peeking around the corner, Tom found Noel in the kitchen. The presence of others in his house felt completely foreign, but he could tell that they were just as uncomfortable as he was.

Noel turned around to meet his eyes when the floorboards creaked behind her. "Can we talk?"

He gave her a slow nod, already dreading the conversation.

She walked past him through the living room and into the entryway.

Tom noticed her look over to Holly's old end table, covered in dust, before she stepped through the front door. He followed her and closed the door, making sure the kids weren't right behind them ready to listen in. Then he waited as Noel paced the front yard, looking over the patches of grass.

"I see the yard is *different* than the way Mom had it," she finally said after turning around.

Tom exhaled a deep breath at the mention of Holly, knowing what the comment was really about. He turned away, unable to meet her eyes. "Noel, I don't know how many times I have to apologize for what happened." It'd been two years since they'd gone through this routine, and for two years he'd tried to push the memories of those conversations away.

"Then why won't you explain to me what *really* happened?"

"I've told you a hundred times, Noel!" he snapped. "It was a car accident. Simple as that."

"But that doesn't add up! You're the safest driver I know, what with your twenty-two-mile-an-hour rule. And the officer on scene said you told him no one else was on the road, so why won't you tell me the truth?"

Tom finally looked up to meet her eyes. "There is no more to tell. We've gone over this; I lost control and crashed. Is that why you came? You wanted to rehash the past?"

She grimaced in anger. "No."

"Then why did you come? Last time I saw you, you said you didn't ever want to see my disgusting face again."

Noel looked out into the distance. "I told you on the phone; Bryan and I split up. It was originally his house, so he kept it in the divorce. We have nowhere else to go."

"But what happened?" Tom asked. "Did he do something to you?"

"It's complicated, and I just want to move on. If you aren't going to let us stay, then we'll find somewhere else." Her chin began to quiver and she quickly looked down, clearly trying to conceal it. He knew this was difficult for her, but he was flustered too. This was his house, after all, and he needed answers.

"You're just going to come back after two years and ask to stay without any real explanations?"

"Fine. I knew this was a bad idea. We'll just go. I'll find someplace else." She marched past him and reached for the door.

"Noel," he called and waited for her to turn around to look at him. Two years ago, when she'd told him she'd never see him again, he'd believed that she'd meant it. Tom knew she wouldn't have come to him, of all people, unless she truly had no place else to go. "You can stay. But this isn't some sort of hotel. I ain't no maid service or nothing like that. That means those kids have to be clean, quiet, and stay out of my hair. You hear me?"

Noel smiled softly in gratitude. "I hear you. Thanks, Tom."

There it was again, *Tom*. He nudged the dirt at his feet.

"How long were you planning on staying?" Tom asked.

"A few weeks at most. Long enough to find a job and apartment."

A few weeks? He'd expected her to say a couple of days. This was already looking like a bad decision on his part. He liked his life the way it was—alone. A couple of days he could force himself to handle, but weeks? And with Christmas around the corner, the last thing he wanted was more reminders.

"How about this?" Noel said, as though she could sense his hesitation. "I know how much you hate Christmas. We'll be out by December 24."

Tom considered it, then nodded. "Fine. No longer than the twenty-fourth. I can't afford to be supporting all of you. I have bills to pay. And there sure as heck won't be any celebration of Christmas in my house."

"Okay, I promise we'll be out within twenty-four days. I have an interview down at the old printing press set up for tomorrow. I did some calling around about jobs yesterday. I also called to get the kids signed up for school. I'll drop them off in the mornings, and we'll do our best to stay out of your hair."

Tom simply shrugged. What did she expect him to say? Don't worry? She could stay as long as she needed? They both knew that wasn't true. Tom could barely afford to live here himself, so there was no way he could afford four other people. His medical bills these days hadn't been cheap, and if things kept up like they had been much longer, he'd have to move. If Noel really was going to move back to town, then she was right; she needed a job, and they needed to find a place to stay. Simple as that.

Noel and the kids brought their boxes in and unpacked while Tom stayed outside in the yard, doing his best to avoid them. He peered in through the window, however, watching as more and more stuff piled up in his house.

Eventually, after pacing his front yard for the fifteenth time, he couldn't stop thinking about Noel pointing out his neglected lawn, so he turned on the hose and let the water cascade into the grass. He'd given up on it months ago, and because of that, the neighbors had silently collaborated on ways to make him water it, since he was the only one on the entire street without an impeccable front yard. The ones who had been there long enough knew there was no changing his mind, just as they'd never been able to convince him to remodel. To Tom, it was more a matter of principle—he wasn't going to be told what to do. Without a homeowners' association, he had the right to do whatever, or in his case, not do whatever he wanted.

"I never thought I would see the day," a raspy old voice called out.

Tom looked up to see Richard across the brick wall holding the leash of his fluffy white dog, Christie, with her tongue hanging out of the side of her mouth.

"You better not open that big mouth to anyone about this," Tom snapped. "If they ask, it was the rain."

"Easy there, Turbo. Your secret's safe," Richard assured him as Christie barked a few times. "Why are you watering that dang lawn anyway? It's as good as gone."

"No reason, just thought I would see what happens."

"And my name is Moses." Richard chuckled at his own joke. Christie let out another bark. "Oh, stop your yapping, Christie."

"You better get to that walk," Tom said. "Christie's getting impatient."

Richard reached down slowly to pet Christie, causing her to wag her tail with excitement. "I may be slow but I ain't *slow*. It's Noel that's got you doing this, isn't it?"

Tom looked up and held a finger to his lips to tell Richard to shut up. Richard smiled wide, seeing that he'd guessed right.

"How long are they staying? Are you guys talking now?"

Tom narrowed his eyes on Richard in a glare. "Keep your voice down. She promised they'd be out before Christmas. And for your information, I'm not sure if we are talking or not. She's here, but she's still calling me Tom."

Richard shook his head. "She'll come around. You need to just tell her the truth. And hey, aren't you supposed to be at the hospital for insulin treatment about now?"

"Oh, mind your own business, Richard, and get on your way. Get!" Tom snipped.

Richard grinned, then walked off with Christie down the street.

Tom looked back at his house, now filled with people for the first time in two years. This wasn't going to be easy.

HAPTER 2

WEDNESDAY, DECEMBER 2

Noel hadn't slept for even a minute. The worries never seemed to stop as she cradled Evan on one side of her and Brittany on the other; the three of them were in the bed she used to sleep on as a kid. Trevor was sleeping on the couch. She couldn't help but wonder if she was doing the right thing. After all, she was uprooting her kids again, for yet another new school and home where they'd have to make new friends. But she had no place else to go, and of all the times for this to happen, it had to be during the Christmas season. The one time of year her kids looked forward to the most. The time when she'd spoil them with presents. The time when everything seemed to be all right. But now she couldn't even afford food, let alone presents. On top of that, she had to find a job and place to live by December 24. At least she already had an interview lined up for this morning.

After the kids were all dressed and fed, the two youngest said their goodbyes to Tom and Noel dropped them all off at their new schools on her way to her interview. Tom hadn't offered much in the way of a greeting when they'd arrived yesterday, but what had she expected? That's what he'd become since her mom's passing, a grumpy and rude old man. She hated that, of all the people she had to turn to when she was at her rock bottom, it had to be Tom.

All the friends she thought she'd made in Sacramento weren't actually friends at all. Turned out their spare bedrooms were magically being used, even though she knew that just weeks ago they hadn't been.

After two full years, coming home to Glenn Hills was far more difficult than she ever could have imagined. Besides the memories of her mother's death and funeral, being back was also a constant reminder of what once was. Tom had been a different person way back when. Her dad. The supportive man who took her for ice cream every Friday after school. The man who worked hard to support his family. The man who kissed her mom every time he walked through the door, showing Noel what love should look like. The man who went out of his way to make every birthday and holiday special. Even Christmas. He was always trying to outdo himself and his neighbors every year for a shot at the Christmas Cup Competition. He'd stay out in the yard for twelve hours a day until his display was complete while Noel and Holly baked Christmas cookies and decorated the tree. Tom had never won the competition, but that didn't matter to Noel. She'd simply loved seeing the glistening lights that brought with them a magic that made their home feel like their own personal winter wonderland. All traces of that man were gone now.

Back in those days, home was just about the only place she'd wanted to be. In high school she wasn't a popular kid and had certainly taken her fair share of bullying. "Quiet VanHansen" had been her nickname, coined by some of the popular girls. She dreamed of the day she'd finally be able to leave Glenn Hills for college to pursue her dreams of being a doctor, but life had other plans.

Jacob had moved in a few doors down during her senior year of high school. She hadn't exactly been considered a catch by the boys at school. When the popular girls had flocked to him, it was a great surprise to her that he'd bypassed all of them to sit with Noel, who had been eating lunch by herself on the steps.

"Mind if I sit?" he'd asked, the reflection of the sun glowing off the side of his buzzed brown hair. He had a swimmer's body and wore a letterman jacket.

Noel hadn't been able to find her words, and after a momentary brain freeze, she'd finally nodded. She'd grinned wide to herself before remembering her braces. But it was too late; he'd seen them. "Braces, huh?"

Noel had nodded, embarrassed. "Samantha and Alice put you up to this, didn't they? Make fun of the quiet girl with braces. I get it."

"What? Who? I'm not making fun of your braces. I think they're cute."

She'd tried to contain her smile as the word hit her, not knowing how to react. *Cute?* A boy thought her braces were cute? It had to be a dream.

"I'm Jacob," he'd said, offering his hand.

She'd studied it for a long moment, expecting the joke to kick in at any second, but it never did.

"Noel," she'd returned, taking his hand.

"That's a unique name."

"My parents got married on Christmas. They thought the name would be fitting."

"I like it. Very pretty."

His gaze had lingered on her, and she'd felt herself blushing uncontrollably.

They'd eaten their lunches in silence until the bell rang, and then they'd set off, each on their own way.

He'd joined her for lunch again the next day.

And the next.

And the next.

Soon he started coming over after school to "study." Or at least that's what they called it, since they'd talked for hours on end about everything and nothing at all.

Then, to Samantha and Alice's displeasure, he'd asked her to prom and was resolute, despite their attempts to talk him out of it.

On prom night, Noel had chosen to stand against the wall for the first few songs, insisting she was okay by herself while Jacob mingled with some of his new friends from the swimming team. Then "At Last" by Etta James had come on, the perfect slow song, and Noel had watched Samantha grab Jacob's hand and pull him onto the dance floor.

She'd turned and darted into the hallway, realizing how foolish she'd been, when a second later a hand touched her shoulder.

"Can I have this dance?" Jacob had asked.

She'd nodded, trying to mask her tears.

He'd taken her hand, while wrapping his other hand around her waist. They'd danced together in the hallway, all by themselves. And she'd never wanted the moment to end.

When the song was over, she'd smiled up at him and found his gaze was already fixed on her. The next second, he leaned in and their lips met. Shock waves had flown through her body, and a warm comfort pulsed from her chest. It was like nothing else mattered. Just him and her. Together.

Jacob had taken a job as a carpenter a few cities away that summer after high school. Soon after, he'd proposed to her on one knee in a crowded expensive restaurant for all to see.

Noel had said yes.

They'd moved in together after the wedding. She'd planned to start school at the local university that fall, but then something happened that'd thrown her another curveball: the test results came back positive. They were pregnant. Nine months later, Trevor had been born.

By the time Brittany and Evan had arrived, Noel had taken up the role of stay-at-home mom. Jacob worked to afford them a decent lifestyle with food on the table, new clothes for the kids a couple of times a year, and even occasional vacations. Through it all, Noel hadn't regretted her life even for a minute. She'd always dreamt of being a doctor, but there was something far more rewarding about being a mother. It was challenging, and every day was a new adventure. Cooking, cleaning, entertaining, driving, caring for injuries and illnesses, teaching them how to walk, talk, read, write, and on and on it went. The duties of being a mother were never-ending. But she knew those skills wouldn't help her now that Jacob wasn't around anymore.

When Jacob died of an extremely fast-spreading cancer, Noel had lost herself, trying to be the mother she knew her kids needed, but spending much of her time in her room, alone. Better to keep her pain to herself and not burden others. It must've been her way of coping, she supposed. His death was still something she didn't let herself think about often. She'd closed herself off to everyone and become extremely lonely. It'd taken her a long time to even consider dating, and when she had started to date again, it was only because she'd met someone who'd reminded her so much of Jacob, the man she missed so dearly: Bryan, the blonde-haired construction worker who loved to swim. When she had met him, she'd thought it was meant to be. She'd convinced herself he was it. Why else would someone so similar to Jacob have found his way into her life? So when he proposed and offered for her and the kids to move in with him after the wedding, it just felt right. It had also been around the same time the life insurance money was nearing its end, and they'd likely lose the house, which had certainly felt like a sign. Like the saying went, one door closes and another opens, or so she'd thought. In the back of her head, she did have doubts, but she had never actually let herself confront those doubts until he finally ended their marriage and left her and the kids on the street. Hindsight is always twenty-twenty. Bryan might have had similar characteristics to Jacob, but he wasn't actually him. What she had with Jacob could never be replaced.

Now she was on her own, and she didn't want to sulk about that fact. She needed to forget about looking for men, put on a smile, and find a job. Thirty-one years old and she hadn't had a job since high school. She knew she wouldn't be an ideal candidate, but hopefully her interviewer would see being a mother was hard work and should count as legitimate job experience.

Noel parked outside the old printing press, a decrepit wood building that looked like it'd been around since the fifties. Several cars and trucks filled the parking lot. A man on a ladder held up a strand of Christmas lights for another man on the roof to grab.

Ah, the Christmas Cup Competition was alive and well. These days it appeared that everyone was getting in on the action. Except for her scrooge of a father, of course. She smiled politely at the man on the ladder and then smoothed the wrinkles out of her floral dress. Nerves made her stomach begin to churn. Inside the building, the smell of burning wood was pungent. She wasn't sure she liked it, but smells were the last thing she should be complaining about. She needed money.

"Oh, hello there," said an elderly woman at a desk to her left, grinning wide and peering through her glasses.

"Hello," Noel returned, extending her hand for the woman to take while returning the smile. "Are you Ms. Anthony? I'm Noel VanHansen."

"Oh, no, dear. My name is Anne. I'm the receptionist. Are you one of the applicants?"

Noel's heart sank just a little. *Applicants.* Plural.

"Yes, I suppose I am."

"Great, dear. I'll just let Ms. Anthony know you are here. You said your name was Rebecca?"

"Sorry, no, it's Noel VanHansen," Noel corrected.

"Ah, yes. Thank you, dear. Rebecca was the one before. Sorry about that."

Noel nodded and smiled politely, but she suddenly didn't feel so good about her chances.

"Yes, Ms. Anthony. Joelle VanHansen is here for you," Anne said into the phone.

"Noel," Noel interrupted.

Anne smiled back at her while holding up a finger, clearly not acknowledging Noel's correction. "Okay, lovely. I'll send her in." Then she hung up the phone and stood from her desk.

"Ms. Anthony is ready for you, dear. Best of luck." Anne gestured toward the door behind her.

"Thank you" was all Noel could say. Her heart began to beat through her chest, and her hands suddenly felt clammy.

Then she made her way to the door and knocked.

"Come in," a woman called from behind the door.

Noel twisted the handle and pushed the door open. Inside, a red-headed woman, probably mid-forties and slightly overweight, stood behind her desk, her eyes fixed on Noel, expressionless.

"Ms. Anthony?" Noel asked.

"Yes, come in," Ms. Anthony said, her voice curt and direct. "Shut the door behind you."

The office was too small to even be considered homey. One window looked out to the parking lot. A wood desk had papers spewed across it. Two stiff-looking wood-backed chairs and an American flag in the corner completed the ensemble.

Noel strode across the room and reached her hand out for a handshake.

Ms. Anthony took it, shook once, and then let it go. "Have a seat, Ms. VanHansen, was it?"

"Yes, Noel. Pleasure to meet you."

Ms. Anthony nodded. She glanced down at the papers spread across her desk, as though she were looking for something. Noel couldn't help but steal a glance as she sat and realized right away what they were—resumes. Dozens of resumes.

Ms. Anthony looked up after flipping through a few. "Noel VanHansen, you said?"

Noel smiled, trying to stay positive. "Yes, ma'am."

"I don't believe I saw your resume. Did you submit it yet?"

Noel felt her smile dim, probably stopping just shy of a frown. "No, I didn't. I apologize. I didn't know a resume was required."

"Oh, yes, we certainly need a resume if we want to consider hiring you. Surely Anne mentioned it when she set up the interview. Do you have it with you?"

"No, I uh—" Noel hesitated. Anne definitely hadn't mentioned it, but then again, Anne seemed a bit all over the place. "Well, I don't have one."

Ms. Anthony stared for a moment as if Noel had just spoken Japanese.

"I don't have much actual work experience, per se," Noel continued. "See, I've been a stay-at-home mother for the past twelve years, taking care of my three kids. I promise you I am a hard worker and I learn very quickly. I will—"

Ms. Anthony raised a hand to cut her off. "I'm sorry, Ms. VanHansen. We really need someone with more experience. And at the very least, we need a resume."

Noel considered trying to plead her case. She really needed this job, and it was her only bite, but it wasn't worth it. There was no winning this woman over. Instead, Noel simply nodded. "Thank you for your time, Ms. Anthony."

The woman didn't reply.

Noel stood and strode back out the door, embarrassed. She'd made a fool of herself and she wanted the moment to end as quickly as possible.

"How'd it go, dear?" Anne asked as soon as she closed the door.

"Probably not a fit," Noel said. "Thanks for your help."

"Oh, I'm sorry, dear. Good luck out there, and Merry Christmas!"

Noel took a deep breath and made her way through the parking lot as quickly as possible. She got in her van and closed her eyes, resting her head on the steering wheel. She picked up her phone, looking for someone to talk to, but the only person that might understand was Bryan, the one who'd ended things with *her*. Her finger hovered over the call button for several moments before she finally pressed it down.

His answering machine picked up after four rings. "You know what to do," his recording said.

"Bryan," Noel started, but no more than a second later, she hung up.

She lifted her head from the steering wheel and started the car.

It was the first chance Tom had to watch western movies alone and uninterrupted since Noel and the kids had moved in. He sat back into the recliner and grabbed for the remote.

Just as he was getting into the first film, he heard a car pull into the driveway.

He looked down at his watch to see that it had only been an hour. Home already? How could that be? Noel was supposed to be out most of the day looking for jobs. Had she found one? Tom smiled at the thought.

The door sprang open and Noel walked in, her head down. She gave him a soft smile but then continued on. He could see her shoulders slump ever-so-slightly as she rounded the hallway.

Had something happened?

The door closed in the other room.

Then the house went quiet once again. He contemplated asking her what had happened, but then thought better of it. They weren't on those types of terms anymore.

He flipped open the footrest of the recliner and turned the TV on. When he looked over to the screen, he expected to see another western playing on his favorite station. Instead, he found some sort of made-for-TV Christmas movie starting. "What is this garbage?" he said and pressed the clicker to turn the television off. He leaned back in his chair and shut his eyes.

"Grandpa!"

Tom's heart leapt as he shot up in the recliner. He blinked his eyes open as he looked around the room. A second later, two small figures came into focus. Brittany and Evan ran toward him from the back door. Noel and Trevor lingered in the kitchen. He looked at the clock to see it was after 3 p.m. already. He'd napped for over five hours.

"Home from school already?" He wasn't sure how he was supposed to respond. Seeing the kids brought back memories of when they were even younger, him holding them in his arms, him taking them to the park. But then he remembered the vow he'd made to himself after losing Holly. He had to stay at a distance; it was the only way.

"Yeah, it was great!" Evan exclaimed. "Mrs. Johnson said I'm bubbly."

Brittany chimed in next. "Mrs. Wright taught us cursive. She said I'm a natural."

In the background, Trevor opened the fridge. Tom couldn't see him, but he knew that Trevor would be disappointed with what he found.

"Are you freaking kidding me? Mom, Tom has nothing in the fridge," Trevor said, loud enough for Tom to overhear.

The kid had some nerve. Noel calling him by his first name was one thing, but Trevor was a kid, and kids needed to show respect.

"His name is 'Grandpa' to you," Noel rebutted. "And don't worry, I'll pick up some food later."

"Why do I have to call him Grandpa? You call him Tom."

"Because I'm the adult. Now watch your manners."

Trevor didn't say another word.

The boy has become a punk, Tom thought. He flipped the television back on, and, to his luck, a cowboy movie appeared on screen.

Brittany and Evan climbed onto the couch and stared toward the box.

Noel walked back into the living room a moment later.

"Mom?" Evan asked.

"Yes, honey?"

Tom considered asking them to step into the other room so that they wouldn't interrupt his TV time, but he decided to wait another minute to see if they'd quiet down on their own.

"Are we having Christmas this year?"

Tom stole a glance up at Noel. She knew how he felt talking about Christmas in his house.

"Of course, honey, why would you ask that?"

"Because we don't live at home anymore," Evan said. "Santa won't know where to go."

"We'll have a new house soon, and Santa always knows where to go," Noel assured him. "Don't you worry about that."

Evan nodded his understanding but then asked, "Will there be lots of presents?"

Tom stole another glance at Noel, who seemed to be trying her best to avoid his gaze.

"Remember, Evan, Christmas isn't about presents."

That seemed to be enough to silence him. Finally, Tom could focus his attention back on the movie.

"Mom?" Brittany asked.

For crying out loud, Tom thought.

"Yes, sweetie?" Noel asked.

"What's the Christmas Cup Competition?"

Noel waited a moment before answering. "Where'd you hear about that?"

"School," Brittany replied. "All the kids were talking about how they were going to win."

"Me too!" Evan screamed excitedly. "Everyone told me too!"

"It's a contest to see who has the best decorated house for Christmas," Noel explained.

"Can we join the contest, Mom?"

"Yeah, can we?" Evan pleaded.

Noel looked to Tom.

"No. I don't celebrate Christmas," Tom snapped, his blood pressure starting to rise. "Now can you all be quiet? Can't you see the TV is on?"

He turned back to the TV, hoping it would be the end of the conversation. For a long moment, everyone was silent. Then Brittany interrupted again.

"No Christmas, Mom?" Brittany asked.

Tom couldn't take it a second longer. He started to grumble something under his breath but stopped himself. He bolted up from his chair instead, pressing the gizmo to turn off the TV. He stomped into the kitchen. It was time for another peanut butter, mayonnaise, and honey sandwich. Not quite what the doctor ordered, but who cared? He wanted sugar, and that was that. It was better his diabetes progressed faster anyway. For that matter, who cared if he missed his regular doctor's appointments and therapy? Maybe then he'd finally be reunited with Holly. Once he finished putting together the sandwich, Tom marched out the front door. It was time for a long walk, alone.

The sun would soon be setting, and there was already a nip in the air that made Tom regret not grabbing a jacket on his way out. It was too late to go back now though. He didn't want to hear any more talk of Christmas or the Christmas Cup Competition. All he wanted was for the next few weeks to be over already. His decision to let them stay seemed like more and more of a mistake with every passing minute.

Before Tom even made it three houses down, one of his neighbors called to him.

"Hi, Thomas. Merry Christmas!"

He turned to see the thirty-something-year-old woman whose name he'd forgotten. She and her husband had brought him cookies when they'd first moved in a few months back. Tom had eaten them all right, but he hadn't offered anything in the way of a thanks. He hadn't asked them to bring the cookies, after all, had he?

The woman waved enthusiastically while smiling and holding up a wreath in her other hand. Dozens of boxes were strewn across her yard. She'd clearly started her preparations for the Christmas Cup Competition.

Tom continued on without a word. Why couldn't everyone just leave him alone?

CHAPTER 3

THURSDAY, DECEMBER 3

Twenty-two days to find a job and place to live.

Noel dropped the kids off at school, ready for another shot at the job hunt. She hadn't been prepared for the printing press, but hopefully she wouldn't repeat that mistake. Yes, she'd second-guessed both her decision to move back as well as her ability to get a job, but after a couple of hours, she realized Bryan wasn't going to call back and that she was in this alone, with no other options. So she pushed it out of her memory and moved on. After several hours of rewrites on Tom's ancient computer, she'd finally finished her resume, deciding, in the end, to talk about her skills rather than experience. She hoped that someone would be able to relate to the hard work that comes with being a mother.

A light sprinkle began to hit against her windshield, giving the morning a wintry feel. She drove through downtown Glenn Hills as several shop owners were putting up wreaths, lights, garland, and decorations outside their windows. Everyone was preparing for the famous Christmas Cup Competition. Noel couldn't help but smile as she drove by people talking with one another, wearing sweaters, scarves, and gloves. Everything had the makings of a magical winter wonderland that brought with it all of those fond memories from her childhood and teenage years.

She pulled into a parking slot in front of Nina's, a boutique women's clothing store at the end of the street. A "Help Wanted" sign was displayed in the front window for all to see. Noel had seen the job posting online yesterday, and when she'd called about it, the woman on the other end told her to come in the morning with a resume. So, here she was.

Beyond the glass window, Noel noticed a woman hanging garland around the doorway. With no one else in sight, Noel assumed it had to be Nina herself.

Noel pressed the wrinkles out of the same floral dress she'd worn the day before, then shut the car door behind her. She didn't exactly have a plethora of nice clothes, and the dress was the nicest thing she owned.

She put on a smile as the misty sprinkles brushed lightly against her face. The woman behind the window noticed Noel a moment later and waved her in. She looked to be around Noel's age, with a thin, pretty face and fringe bangs, and she wore an elegant gray wool sweater and jeans.

"You must be Noel?" the woman asked, in a much more pleasant tone than Ms. Anthony had the day before.

"Yes. Nina, I take it?"

"Yes. Great to meet you." Nina offered a limp handshake, and Noel took it.

"Likewise. I really appreciate you meeting with me."

Nina set down the garland she'd been working around the doorway and gestured toward two leather chairs beside the rows of clothing. Noel took note of the designer blouses and sweaters. There couldn't have been more than fifty items of clothing in the entire store, but Noel guessed the profits didn't come from volume. Based on the concrete floors, exposed brick walls, and colorful mannequins, Noel assumed that this was a high-scale boutique. Probably not the type of clothes she'd be able to afford, but she wasn't here to shop; she was here for a job.

They took their seats across from one another.

Noel's hands shook slightly as she reached into her purse for her resume.

Noel knew Nina took note of the shaking. "Oh, great, let's take a look," she said as she grabbed the paper.

Noel smiled politely as Nina studied it. She considered speaking but decided to wait until Nina was done.

After a long moment, Nina glanced up, looking confused at first, but then she laughed.

Noel took it as a good sign and couldn't help but laugh as well.

Nina finished with an amused smile. "I've certainly never seen a resume like this before. It's funny."

Noel's smile faded slightly. "Funny?"

"Yes, it's a joke, right? Trying to get my attention with a laugh?"

Noel stared, unsure whether or not she was serious. "What do you mean by a *joke?*"

Nina studied her. "There isn't any experience listed on here. It's all qualifications. Surely this isn't serious?"

Noel took a moment to compose herself and kept a measured tone. "It's very serious. I'm a mother. I've been one for twelve years. I don't have any job experience, but I can assure you I'm more than qualified."

Nina looked down, smiling to herself. "I'm sorry. I don't think this is going to work out here."

Noel nodded and, without another word, bolted through the store and out the door. The misty sprinkles had turned to a more steady rain. Noel took deep breaths, trying to stay calm as several shop owners glanced in her direction.

Nina had undoubtedly been rude, but Noel needed to shake it off and move past it.

It wasn't meant to be, she told herself.

Noel looked down the street, wondering if any of the other shops might be hiring. There were dozens of stores and businesses downtown, so surely someone had to be. She wiped the tears away. Then she marched down the sidewalk until she reached Glenn Hills Realty.

Sure enough, a "Help Wanted" sign hung on the door. A white snowflake mural was painted on the window, with an igloo and what looked like the North Pole on the far right. Beyond the winter wonderland, she saw several people already sitting at desks inside.

She took a nervous breath, then she opened the door. Several faces looked up at her as she walked in. "Hello," she announced. "Sorry to interrupt, but I saw the 'Help Wanted' sign in the window."

A young man with a shaved head stood. He couldn't have been over twenty years old. "Yes. We're looking for an appointment setter." He offered a hand. "I'm Olie, the office manager."

Noel smiled as she took it. "Noel. Pleasure to meet you."

He smiled back. "Do you happen to have a resume with you?"

Noel dug into her purse and pulled another one out, grateful she'd printed a few copies. It was slightly crumpled, and she tried to straighten it quickly before handing it over.

"Great." He looked down at the resume while several of the others slowly directed their attention back to their computers. A moment later, he looked back up. "I'm sorry, Ms. VanHansen. It doesn't look like you have any experience. We're looking for at least three years in a similar position."

"Well, I don't have job experience per se, but I've been a mother for twelve years. I can assure you I can get the job done."

Noel noticed a couple of women snickering and smirking at one another a few desks down.

"I'm sorry, but I don't think that you are the best fit for the position." Olie offered a sympathetic smile. "But good luck. I'm sure you'll find a job somewhere else."

A kid, who couldn't be older than twenty years old, was turning her down for her lack of experience. Where was she supposed to get experience if low-level jobs wouldn't even take her?

Noel didn't look back as she turned and walked through the door, but she had a feeling the women were laughing it up at her expense. Part of her wanted to march back in there and tell them how rude they'd been. Tell them how hard it is being a single mother. But instead, she let out a long breath and pressed on.

Outside, the rain fell harder than it had a few minutes before. The shop owners that had been outside decorating were now indoors. She glanced across the street, trying not to let the situation get to her, reminding herself that she'd probably never see them again, and that maybe one day when they had kids they'd understand what it was like to be in her shoes. Then she crossed the street, wishing she'd brought an umbrella. She hoped her resumes weren't getting wet inside her purse.

Across the street, she passed Bertha's Diner, Tom's favorite restaurant. The windows had an immaculate and intricate snowflake mural strewn with flakes of differing shapes and sizes on them. Inside, several patrons ate their breakfasts in happy conversation. In the back, she saw Bertha herself, carrying some plates over to a couple in the back. Bertha wore a red apron and her short, curly white hair bounced as she walked. Her rosy red cheeks looked radiant, and Noel couldn't help but notice that Bertha looked exactly the same after all these years. Bertha had been a friend of her mom's, and had even brought baked goods by once in a while when Noel was a teen.

Their gazes met when Bertha glanced up. It took a second for Bertha to recognize Noel, but when she did, she waved her in.

Bertha set down the plates for the couple, then moved toward her, reaching out her arms for a hug. "Noel! If it isn't the most beautiful woman in town," Bertha said, loud enough for everyone to hear.

Several patrons looked over as Noel leaned in for a hug.

For the slightest of seconds, Noel envisioned her mom in her arms instead of Bertha, yearning for the moment to be real, but she pushed the image away the very next second. Her mom wasn't there anymore, and there wasn't anything she could do about it now.

"Thank you, Bertha," she said as they embraced. "So nice to see you."

Bertha put her hands on her hips when they released. "Tom didn't tell me you were back in town. How the heck are ya?"

"Oh, I'm okay. How about you? Still cookin' the best breakfast in Glenn Hills, I see."

"That's what they tell me, so I keep on cooking." Bertha laughed. "Golly gee, I don't think I've seen you since Holly's funeral, rest her beautiful soul. So what brings you to town?"

Noel sighed. "My husband left me, so I'm staying with Tom until I can find a job."

Bertha shook her head and pursed her lips. "Oh, dear."

"Yup," Noel said. "You don't happen to know anyone hiring, do you?"

Bertha looked up for a moment, thinking. "You know what, I think I saw a sign a couple of places down. Glenn Hills Classic Coffee."

Noel perked up. "Really? I may have to check that out."

"Please do. Now why don't you have a seat? I'll whip you up some of your dad's favorite waffles. On the house."

"Oh, no, I couldn't. Thanks, though, Bertha. That's really nice of you."

Bertha narrowed her eyes, as though she were about to contest it, then she softened and let out a jolly laugh. "Okay. But don't be a stranger. You come by anytime."

Noel nodded and smiled. "Thanks, Bertha."

She walked out feeling much better than she had before she'd gone inside. She continued onward to find the coffee shop Bertha had mentioned, past a print shop, candy shop, another realty brokerage, and a hobby shop.

Then she saw it, Glenn Hills Classic Coffee. And sure enough, there was a "Help Wanted" sign in the window.

A Christmas wreath hung on the door. Noel opened it to the strong smell of fresh ground coffee beans and something sweet, like cinnamon rolls baking in an oven. A jazzy rendition of "Jingle Bells" hummed in the background. The lighting was dark, giving the exposed brick shop a moody feel. Several people sat inside, working on computers or tablets while sipping coffees or nibbling on scones and pastries.

"What can I do for you?" a strong, deep voice asked from across the shop.

Noel glanced toward the counter to see a man in a red flannel standing behind it. He was rugged, with a burly but trimmed light brown beard, and short brown hair slicked to the side. Certainly good looking in an outdoorsy man's man type of way. Probably a few years older than her. Noel stopped herself from sizing him up right there. His looks didn't matter, and she needed to stop sizing men up anyway. She needed to focus on herself and her kids, which meant looking past this man's looks and simply focusing on getting a job. Plus, he was probably about to embarrass her anyway by giving her another harsh rejection because of her lack of qualifications.

"I saw the 'Help Wanted' sign in the window," she finally said.

"Ah, yes. We're looking for a barista. Do you have a resume by chance?"

Noel took a deep breath, then reached into her purse and pulled one out. Several water splotches soaked the page, smearing the ink in places. "Shoot, looks like it's a bit wet." She quickly tried to blot it out with a napkin on the counter.

"That's quite all right. Let's have a quick look."

When he held out his hand for the resume, Noel noticed a gold wedding band on his ring finger. Married. Figures. She knew she shouldn't have been checking him out anyway.

He smiled a friendly smile as she handed him the resume, then he began to skim through it. The smile grew wider as he went, and immediately Noel realized she'd made a mistake. It was pointless. And then, as the icing on the cake, he laughed.

"I'll just go," Noel announced as she turned and walked back toward the door, upset with herself and filled with embarrassment again. Several of the patrons looked up from their devices at the scene.

"Wait," he called. "Where are you going, Ms. VanHansen? Or is it Mrs. VanHansen?"

"Ms. And don't worry. Just laugh it up. I get it. You need more experience," she said, opening the door.

"That's not why I'm laughing."

Noel turned back to the man, who was still smiling. "Oh yeah? What was it about then?"

"You're a mother, right?"

Noel was certain she hadn't put that on the resume. She didn't answer, skeptical at what he was getting at.

"You don't need a resume for that. Being a mother is the hardest job there is. How many kids do you have?"

Was he being serious? The burly man's man was the one to appreciate what it meant to be a mother? It still felt like some sort of gimmick.

"Three," Noel said. "Do you have kids yourself?"

"Nope. I wish we did, though."

She studied him.

"The name's Tate." He held a hand over the counter for her to shake.

Noel hesitated at first, but then took it. It was soft and warm, but firm. A second later they let go.

"Noel," she returned.

"I own the place and could definitely use the help," Tate said. "When can you start?"

Noel tilted her head, perplexed by the question. "Are you saying I have the job? You know nothing about me."

"Like I said, being a mom is a tougher job than any other. You are looking for a job, and I need the help. As long as you don't mind going home smelling like coffee, it's fifteen dollars an hour plus tips. We can work around your schedule. Sound okay?"

Noel watched him, waiting for the joke to fall into place, but it never did. He was serious. Energizing shockwaves pulsed through her veins. She couldn't contain her smile.

She'd done it! She'd gotten a job!

"Sounds wonderful! You won't regret it."

Fifteen dollars an hour plus tips was even better than she could have hoped from her very first job. Plus, working around her schedule was more than generous. And she loved coffee and cooking.

"I have a good feeling about you," Tate said with a narrow grin. "I'm heading out soon and another barista, Josephine, will be taking over for me, but can you come in tomorrow to fill out the paperwork and learn the ropes? She's young but she knows it all, and you'll be in good hands. Say eight or so?"

Noel beamed. "That'd be perfect."

"Great." Tate turned to face the patrons in the store. "Dignified coffee drinkers," he announced for everyone to hear. He gestured toward her when they turned to look in his direction. "I want to introduce you to our newest barista, Noel."

Noel felt her cheeks immediately flush from the attention.

"Hi, Noel," someone called back. A few others shouted their own greetings, and several nodded while smiling.

"They love you already," Tate said.

Noel laughed. "Thanks for that. And thanks for the job. I won't let you down."

Tate nodded, his eyes fixed on her. "Looking forward to working with you, Noel."

She smiled back. "Me too. See you tomorrow."

"See you then."

Noel turned and strolled casually out the door, trying to contain her excitement. She waved as she exited the door into the rain, and the moment she turned the corner, she felt like her face would burst from her electric grin.

Tom stared out at the constant rain beating against the grass in the backyard. Northern California wasn't the best climate for greenery. Winters were often just as warm and dry as summers. But this year appeared to be different. It was the first rain of the season, and it showed no signs of stopping. Tom wondered what the residents of Glenn Hills would do about their beloved Christmas Cup Competition. Surely the rain would be a deterrent for anyone looking to decorate outside.

Noel's minivan pulled into the driveway, and Tom contemplated grabbing an umbrella and heading out, but decided the rain was coming down too hard. At least he'd have an excuse to tell the doctor about why he couldn't get his walking in. And for that matter, why he couldn't make it to the grocery store to pick up healthier food. He had noticed some new additions in the fridge, no doubt from Noel for the kids. He didn't like all the extra stuff around, throwing off the order to his chaos.

Tom rushed into the kitchen to put together a peanut butter, mayonnaise, and honey sandwich, then he hurried toward his bedroom as fast as he could, but he didn't make it before Noel and the kids opened the door.

"Grandpa!" Evan shouted, sprinting toward him and clutching onto his waist.

Tom grunted.

Brittany ran in and hugged his waist as well. "Look what I made!" She held up a circular ornament, painted with sloppy red splotches.

"Well, you can't put it up here," he replied. "There will be no tree in my house."

"But it's a Christmas ornament," Brittany protested. "For Santa!"

"We can't get a tree, Mom?" Evan asked.

Noel walked in from behind them, with a radiance in her eyes Tom hadn't seen since she'd been back. Trevor lingered behind her in silence. "I don't know, honey," she said, obviously a subject she wanted to avoid, then she looked up at Tom. "I have good news, Tom."

"Oh?"

She spread her lips into a wide grin. "I got a job! Down at Glenn Hills Classic Coffee. I start tomorrow."

Tom didn't know what to say. A job meant that they'd be able to move out. And it meant less financial burden for both him and Noel. But what would she do with the kids while she had to work? Luckily tomorrow was Friday, which meant there was school, but what about weekends when she wasn't around? "Good," he finally said.

"I was wondering if maybe the kids might be able to stay with you for a bit after school tomorrow? Going forward I'll make sure my schedule aligns with theirs as best as I can."

There it was, the question he'd been dreading. What was he supposed to do with three kids? "Well, uh—" he started.

"Please, Tom. I promise they will be on their best behavior, and we'll be out of your hair soon enough, once I can get enough money to put a deposit down for rent somewhere. Should just be a few weeks."

Tom looked down at Brittany and Evan, both beaming up at him, twinkles in their eyes. Trevor watched for Tom's reaction too. Tom tried to avoid all thoughts of vulnerability, the way they each reminded him of Noel as a child. She'd adored him back then, a feeling he hadn't known in years. Part of him wanted to push them away like he was supposed to, but another part longed for the way things had once been.

"Okay, I guess. They have to be on their best behavior though," he warned, "and when the TV is on, that means no talking."

"Yay!" Brittany and Evan yelled, jumping up and down in celebration.

"Thanks, Tom," Noel said.

Tom grunted and turned and walked back to his room to be alone for the rest of the evening. If he was going to have to watch the kids tomorrow after school, he needed some peace and quiet. He flipped on an old western, then he laid back on the bed and ate his sandwich as the rain continued to pour down outside his window, uninterrupted.

Just the way he was used to.

CHAPTER 4

The rain had vanished and the sun was back out for another bright California winter day. To Tom, that meant nothing more than watching westerns on the old TV. But it didn't last long because by the time afternoon rolled around, the school bus dropped the kids off in front of the house. Now that they were officially in their new schools, Noel had been able to get them onto the bus route for the days she was working.

"Can we play in the garage?" Brittany and Evan asked in unison, seconds after they burst through the door.

Trevor stood in the kitchen, waiting for Tom's answer.

Tom looked back, incredulous that they'd interrupted his TV time again. They knew the rules; TV on meant voices off. What could they possibly want in the garage? "Whatever. But be careful!"

"Trevor, can you help us?" Evan asked.

"Yeah," Trevor mumbled.

As the kids disappeared into the garage, Tom refocused his attention on the television once more.

Half an hour passed, but the kids never came back inside.

What in the heavens could they be doing out there for so long?

Tom flipped off the TV. Then he stood up to peer out the window and into the detached garage across the way. Inside, all three kids were standing over a large cardboard box. When Tom leaned closer to see what was inside the box, he realized it was Christmas lights. They'd found his old box of Christmas lights from the years he'd entered the Christmas Cup Competition.

"Gosh dang it!" he yelled as he stomped through the door into the garage. The second he'd opened the door, all three kids had leapt up in front of the box, clearly trying to hide what they were doing. "What's going on in here?" he demanded.

"Nothing!" Trevor said, stepping protectively in front of the other two.

Tom stepped closer to look into the box of lights. "What's this?"

Evan's eyes went wide, and he pursed his lips, trying to keep himself from spilling the beans, but he couldn't handle the pressure. "Christmas lights! It was Trevor's idea!"

Trevor glared at him.

"I said no Christmas lights," Tom fumed. "If you are going to stay here, you listen to my rules. Got it?"

Brittany and Evan nodded their defeat.

Trevor narrowed his eyes.

"Now get back inside."

All three kids walked out of the garage in silence, leaving Tom alone with the open box of lights. He reached down, closed it, and put it back onto the shelf.

Those kids needed to learn a thing or two about respect.

Noel pulled up into the driveway shortly after he'd settled back into his chair.

"Mommy!" Brittany yelled, running to Noel and jumping into her arms.

"Good, I can finally get some rest," Tom sputtered. He practically bolted up from his recliner; then he made his way to the bedroom and out of sight.

The kids were pushing his buttons, what with their efforts to unearth the Christmas lights he'd purposefully kept hidden, which brought back so many of the memories he'd kept locked away. Holly. Her love for Christmas. Their anniversary. The night they'd gone to see Glenn Hills's Christmas displays, and the accident that ripped her away from him for the rest of his days.

It left him with a feeling he hated, the one he'd attempted to avoid for the last two years: vulnerability.

He missed her.

CHAPTER 5

SATURDAY, DECEMBER 5

Tom sat in the kitchen eating a piece of toast and drinking his overly sweetened coffee while watching the rain beat down against the window. Noel approached him soon after he'd finished, wearing a blue dress and white sweater over it. Her cheeks were brushed with a subtle pink makeup, and her blonde hair was down in elegant loose ribbon curls. Clearly the look had taken some time.

"Morning, Tom," she said as she poured herself a glass of orange juice, another new addition to the fridge.

"Morning." He glanced down at his wet Saturday copy of the *Glenn Hills Times*. An article centered on the front page described how the Christmas Cup Competition was already on pace to double any past winnings. The cups around town were filling with donations that could reach as high as fifteen thousand dollars. Tom did a double take to make sure he'd read it right. *Fifteen thousand dollars?*

Back in the days when Tom used to throw his hat in the ring, the winnings had only been a few hundred dollars. That was incentive enough even though he'd never won. In those days, it had always been his nemesis, Phil Bartson, who'd won every year. Phil Bartson was around Tom's age and lived nearby in a twelve-bedroom bamboo oasis, overly lavish even for its time. Their Christmas light display was second to none. Phil boasted the fact that he had over seventy thousand individual bulbs on display. Tom had never even come close, but it wasn't because of a lack of effort. Every year, Tom tried to go bigger and better, outdoing himself and his neighbors. A few years into his attempts, Tom found out that Phil had made nice with several of the city council members who happened to be judges, even going so far as to donate to several of their re-election campaigns. So when Tom received the news he'd lost again, his competitive nature got the better of him. Against Holly's advice, he'd decided to show up at the following city council meeting.

Tom let them have it while they sat in stunned silence.

The following year, Phil didn't win, but neither did Tom. He walked out several times that season to find his light display unplugged, and although he had his suspicions, he could never prove it was Phil who had done it. Eventually the Bartson family moved away, and in all the years after, Tom still never won. He figured that his run-in with the city council had blacklisted him as a potential winner, but he'd tried every year up until the year of Holly's death.

Tom continued to skim the paper when he saw another article about the winner of the competition last year, the Garcetti family. There was a picture of a regal looking Italian family wearing matching red sweaters standing in front of an enormous white marble home. The article went on to talk about how they planned to go even bigger this year, with an entirely new display of lights and decorations. At the bottom of the article, Mr. Garcetti made mention of a garage sale Sunday morning where they would sell all the old lights from the previous years they'd won.

A moment later, Tom heard footsteps.

"Grandpa! Mom! Can I have cereal?" Evan yelled.

Tom cringed, not ready for that volume at this time of the morning.

"Indoor voices, Evan, remember, and sure," Noel said. She grabbed a bowl and poured him some cereal.

Tom wasn't sure how clean those bowls were, but he wasn't going to be the one to say anything.

Brittany walked in a second later, rubbing the sleep out of her eyes. She squinted toward Noel. "Good morning, Mommy. Good morning, Grandpa." Her voice was hoarse.

Noel set another bowl of cereal down on the table. "Good morning, sweetie."

Tom moved over, uncomfortable with how close they all were. He glanced back at his newspaper, looking for something to get him out of talking.

"Trevor, cereal," Noel called as she set a third bowl on the table.

Trevor walked in, again wearing all black, with his hair already spiked tall.

Tom didn't understand the kid's fashion. Was it the cool thing these days? To Tom, Trevor looked more like a porcupine than anything else.

Trevor glared silently at Tom and then sat down. A moment later, all three kids dug into their cereal. The metal from their spoons clanked against the bowls between each loud and obnoxious slurp.

Tom lifted his newspaper even higher, trying to block them out completely.

"Grandpa," Brittany beckoned from across the table.

Didn't anyone understand what silence at breakfast meant? Tom lowered his newspaper to meet her eyes.

Brittany spooned a giant bite of cereal into her mouth. "Mom said we had to ask you if it was okay," she muttered.

"Ask me what?" Tom snapped.

"If we can enter the Christmas Cup Competition."

"Yeah, Grandpa!" Evan exclaimed, jumping from his seat. "Can we?"

"Evan, inside voices," Noel interjected. She looked up to meet Tom's eyes. "Tom, I meant to ask you." She started washing out her bowl, then continued speaking when Tom laid his newspaper down. "Well, with Christmas coming and all, and now that I'll be working . . ." She paused, clearly trying to find her words. "I know how much you hate Christmas, but I'm not sure how much I can prevent it. Everyone at school is talking about the Christmas Cup Competition, and you see, Christmas is their favorite time of year. It was Jacob's too, and it's always just been a special time."

"What are you saying?" Tom sputtered.

"I'm saying that we'll be out by the twenty-fourth, like I promised, so we won't be here for Christmas day, but I can't let my kids go without the holiday, even though you don't want to acknowledge Christmas. It's one of the last pieces of Jacob they have left to hold onto. We can avoid talking about it around you, but I am not going to stop them from celebrating it. As difficult as it might be financially, I need to make it special for them." She paused again. "Look, the kids really want to enter the Christmas Cup Competition. I know I've already asked a lot of you, and I know how much you hate it. All I am hoping is that you might consider it. For them. Maybe you could look at it as more of a competition than a Christmas celebration." Her posture stiffened once she'd finished her rambling, as though she were waiting to see how Tom would protest.

Brittany and Evan's eyes were glued to Tom, eagerly awaiting his response. Even Trevor watched for his reaction.

Tom waited another moment before finally replying, "Okay." Then he went back to reading his newspaper.

"Really?" Evan jumped up and hugged Brittany in excitement.

Noel stared at Tom in shock, completely thrown off by his response. It seemed she'd expected to have to argue her case. But she'd said what she needed to say, and he'd complied. He knew that she knew him well enough not to press it any further. "Okay, great. Well, I'm off to the coffee shop. You sure you'll be okay with the kids?"

"Mmhm," Tom grunted without looking up.

Noel shrugged to herself.

"Trevor, I need you to keep an extra eye on the kids too, and if Tom does decide to enter the Christmas Cup Competition, then you have to do whatever he asks."

"Whatever," Trevor said.

Tom wanted to say something about respect, but he stopped himself.

He knew he'd surprised Noel and the kids by agreeing to consider the Christmas Cup Competition, and frankly, he'd surprised himself too. But it wasn't just Noel and the kids that had changed his mind. Seeing the article about the Garcettis had fired him up, bringing back memories of all those years he'd tried and lost the Christmas Cup Competition. Just like the Barstons, the Garcettis were the last family in the city that needed the money. And in Tom's mind, that wasn't right. If there was one thing Tom hated more than Christmas, it was when people were given things because of privilege or money.

Plus, entering the competition was just that, a competition. It didn't mean he had to actually celebrate Christmas. He could simply partici- pate in the competition, like Noel had said, and leave all the rest of the Christmas stuff out. It also didn't hurt that fifteen thousand dollars was on the line.

Tom went back to reading his paper as the children excused them- selves from the table to get dressed for the day.

The rain continued steadily throughout the day. Tom laid back in his recliner while a Clint Eastwood movie played on the television. Brittany and Evan lay napping on the couch, while Trevor sat at the kitchen table, clicking away on his laptop. For the most part, all three kids had been silent for the day, which, in Tom's mind, was exactly how it should be. Then a voice came from behind him:

"Uh, Grandpa?"

Tom jumped up, startled by the unexpected voice. He looked toward the couch and found both Evan and Brittany still asleep. Then he turned back to see Trevor looking down at him from behind. Was he hearing things? Or was Trevor actually talking to him? And had he called him Grandpa?

"Yes, Trevor?"

"I was doing some research on the Christmas Cup Competition and thought you might want to see what some of the top houses did last year." Trevor held up the laptop, as though signaling there was something on the computer he wanted to show Tom.

Tom took a deep breath and then rolled his eyes. "Oh, all right. Let's see it."

Trevor knelt down beside the recliner and balanced the laptop on the armrest for them both to watch.

An image of a house was displayed on the screen. The house wasn't lit up though; in fact, it was dark. Tom squinted to the top to see the website was something called "YouTube." It looked like one of those sites he'd been warned about filled with viruses sure to destroy the computer and steal all the information on it.

"Just press play when you are ready," Trevor offered.

Tom searched the screen for anything that said play, but couldn't find it. "Looks like it's broken."

"It's not broken, Grandpa. You just need to press play." Trevor reached up and touched a gray rectangle below the keyboard.

Suddenly, the computer came to life. Tom wanted to push the dang thing away with all of its stupid controls that no one needed, but a moment later, he was too enthralled.

On the screen, the house stayed dark a second longer, then suddenly music blasted from the computer. The house lit up, nearly every inch covered in electric white lights. The music sounded like some sort of grand symphony, and it took a moment before Tom recognized the melody of "Carol of the Bells." Lights began to twinkle one section at a time while the other sections went dark. Then Tom realized that the song was playing with the rhythm of the lights. Trumpets blared and the entire house burst into light. In all his years as an electrician, Tom had never seen such a thing. He'd seen light shows, but never something as enthralling and electrifying as this. The symphony wound down, and with one more flash of all the lights, the house went dark. The video stopped.

Tom couldn't look away. He tried to compute the wiring and circuitry that would have to be done to pull off something so complex.

"One more to show you. These guys have won the last five years in a row." Trevor pressed a series of keys Tom couldn't make out and repositioned the laptop on the armrest.

Another video of a house came into view. This time, the camera moved forward. Tom squinted, and suddenly the white marble house lit up. Green and red lights strewn across the roof and across pillars, windows, and doors. It looked elegant, but Tom had certainly seen better. In fact, he was certain his own house used to look better. The camera slowly panned along the massive house, when a second later, music began to play.

A child began to sing. "Up on the housetop reindeer pause, out jumps good old Santa Claus." The camera shot to the roof, now illuminated brightly for all to see. Tom would have sworn he hadn't seen anything a moment before, but he knew his eyes weren't deceiving him. On the roof were a red sleigh, two rows of reindeer, and Santa: hat, beard, suit, and all. Tom had to assume the reindeer were fake, but by the way the Santa was moving, Tom had to guess he was real. Santa rose up out of the sleigh and began to wave down to the camera.

"Down through the chimney with lots of toys, all for the little ones Christmas joys," the song continued.

Santa stepped out of the sleigh and then hauled a giant red bag toward the chimney. He looked down again at the camera, climbed up and into the chimney, waved, and disappeared.

"What the—?" Tom said. "Where'd he go?"

The video continued as the music kept on in the background. The cameraman walked toward the side of the house where more lights came into view. A gate covered in green and red stood tall, and above it hung a sign that said "North Pole."

The gate swung open, and several kids screamed with delight, running through it. The cameraman continued behind the chaos of the crowd. Soon, it appeared that they were in the backyard. A cobblestone walkway led the way through rows upon rows of lit Christmas trees. Each one appeared to be decorated in different ways and with different themes: one with all white ornaments, another with all blue ornaments, another with glittery pine cones, another with sea shells, and another with garland. The cameraman continued through the rows of lit trees. When finally the crowd came back into view, everyone was staring toward what looked like a throne on top of hundreds of presents. The music was now a low hum in the background.

Suddenly, silence fell and Santa appeared in front of the throne, standing and waving. "Merry Christmas, everyone. Ho, ho, ho." Everyone burst into cheers and applause. Children lined up the next second and, one by one, approached Santa's lap. Then the video stopped, and Tom finally looked up.

"If we're going to win, we have to beat that," Trevor said. "Just thought you might want to see."

Tom stood up from his seat, flustered from what he'd seen. "There's no need for all that fancy mumbo jumbo music and Santa on the roof. Their house is too big anyway. All you need is lights. Simple as that."

Tom went to the kitchen to be alone, his blood pressure far too high for a lazy Saturday indoors. Noel arrived home a short time later smiling from ear to ear and smelling of coffee. Without even asking how her day had gone, Tom said, "Finally, I can nap," before disappearing for the rest of the night.

CHAPTER 6

SUNDAY, DECEMBER 6

Tom woke up on Sunday morning with a plan.

Noel, Trevor, Brittany, and Evan were already at the kitchen table eating cereal when Tom approached.

"Grandpa!" Evan screamed.

"Evan, how many times do I have to remind you, inside voices," Noel snapped.

"Hi, Grandpa," Brittany added.

"Morning," Tom said.

Trevor didn't acknowledge him as he walked by. It seemed that their moment watching videos together yesterday had already escaped Trevor. Tom felt a pang of surprise and hurt, but then he pushed it away, reminding himself that was how it was supposed to be anyway.

"Morning, Tom," Noel said through a sip of orange juice.

Tom glanced outside to see the rain had finally stopped, giving way to another sunny California winter day, and then he poured himself a cup of coffee, noticing that the coffee maker had already been turned on.

"Oh, I hope you don't mind," Noel said. "Already brewed you a pot, you know, to get my practice in for the shop."

"Hmm," Tom acknowledged.

He didn't like her touching his machine, but he poured himself a cup anyway. Part of him instinctively wanted to thank her, and ask her about her job, but the other part told him it was better not to. "So, Tom," Noel continued, "my second day went pretty good yesterday.

Another gal showed me the ropes while I worked the register. Anyway, they called me a bit ago because they have another shift open for today, and I was wondering if you might be okay with watching the kids again? They told me they had a great time yesterday."

Tom turned to meet her eyes. They told her they had a great time? Brittany and Evan watched Clint Eastwood movies most of the day, while napping the rest, and Trevor had stayed to himself on the computer. But if she said so. "Fine." Tom sat down and drank his coffee. He gave it a double take, surprised by how good it tasted. "Kids, when you finish with breakfast, get your coats. We're going to a garage sale."

They all looked at him skeptically.

"What?" Tom said. "You said you wanted to enter the Christmas Cup Competition, right?"

"Yes!" Evan yelled.

"Yes!" Brittany yelled in agreement.

"Then we need to get some more lights."

Trevor looked to Noel in astonishment, at which Noel smiled and shrugged. Tom lifted his coffee cup back to his lips, and he couldn't help but smile behind it.

Tom glanced over his shoulder to the back seat.

Both Evan and Brittany were securely buckled into their car seats, smiling wide from the back. Trevor, by default, sat in the front and stared out the passenger window.

"Everyone's seat belt on?" Tom asked. He already knew Brittany and Evan were good, so the question was meant for Trevor.

"It's on, Grandpa," Brittany called from behind him.

"Me too!" Evan shouted.

Trevor continued to stare out the window, but after a reluctant second, he casually pulled it over himself and buckled in.

"Good. Let's go." Tom reversed out of the driveway and started down the street.

The Ford Bronco bucked into second gear, accelerating to a safe and comfortable eighteen miles an hour. Trevor gazed over at the speedometer, then raised his eyebrows obnoxiously to show his annoyance. Tom noticed the gesture and decided to slow down to a mere fifteen miles an hour. Trevor scoffed in anger.

"Do you have an issue, Trevor?" Tom asked, a bit more direct than he probably should have been with a child.

Trevor rolled his eyes.

"There is never a need to go over twenty-two miles an hour on a surface road. Take it from me, safe is better than sorry." Tom looked over to Trevor and then took a deep breath.

Tom hated crowds. Normally he kept to himself, and that was how he liked it. Holly had always been the opposite. She'd been the one to make nice with all the neighbors, no matter who they were. Didn't matter if Tom hated them, Holly would always go out of her way to bake cookies and make new friends when people moved to town. Where Tom didn't care if he offended someone, Holly did. And whenever Tom made a fool of himself, like at the city council meeting, Holly would show up afterward with baked goods and an apology on behalf of the family. Tom always reminded her that he wouldn't apologize, but then Holly would remind him that he would unless he wanted to sleep on the couch.

The white marble mansion came into view, not yet decorated for this year's competition. The crowd at the Garcettis' garage sale had to be bigger than any other garage sale in the history of garage sales.

Evan, Brittany, and Trevor followed behind Tom while wearing their winter jackets for the deceptively cold sunny day.

"You didn't tell me we were going to the Garcettis' garage sale," Trevor said from behind him.

Tom continued toward the chaos ahead. Tables went on, far back into the yard, filled with trinkets, clothes, toys, appliances, and anything else one could imagine. "What does it matter if it's the Garcettis' garage sale?"

Trevor rolled his eyes.

Okay then, Tom thought.

Tom made his way past dozens of people of all ages. He was on a mission, scanning one table then another, searching. Finally, the table came into view, and his eyes lit up. Lights. Lots of Christmas lights.

Tom navigated around a crying baby and reached the table. Several boxes of rolled-up fat light bulbs sat on top of the table. He began rummaging through them, counting the strands one by one while Brittany and Evan tried to get on their tiptoes to peek inside. Trevor kept his head down, standing behind him.

After the eighth box, Tom's tally came to one hundred and forty-two strands. There was still the question of whether or not they worked, but he would be sure to bring that up when it came time to haggle. Tom was one for a bargain. Just about every big purchase he'd ever made, he'd haggled. The house, the car, the computer—heck, even the hospital bill for Noel's birth. Granted, he'd always had Holly around to play good cop to his bad cop, a ploy in the art of negotiation. But Tom knew the real reason he'd been able to talk so many prices down was because of his determination.

As such, Tom knew exactly what he needed to do if he was going to get these lights on the cheap. He also knew that if he wanted to buy new lights at the store, the price would be astronomical. Thousands of dollars at a minimum. And Tom didn't have thousands of dollars, what with all the medical bills and lack of income.

"Trevor, can you go find someone working here?" Tom asked.

"Have Brittany do it," Trevor whined.

Tom looked back to see Trevor hiding his head. He normally acted strange, but something had him acting even stranger today.

"Hello there. Can I help you?" a cheery voiced man asked from the other side of the table.

Tom glanced up to see a dapper dark-haired man in a green knit sweater and a teenage girl wearing a matching green sweater standing beside him. Tom recognized them right away. It was the Garcetti family he'd seen in the newspaper.

"Looking at the old light display, I see?" the man asked.

"Huh? Uh, yeah," Tom grunted without returning the smile.

Evan greeted them with an enthusiastic wave. "Hi, I'm Evan."

Tom looked back to see Evan peeking up from behind the table, with Brittany smiling by his side. For a moment Tom couldn't find Trevor, then he realized that Trevor was standing directly behind him. Was he hiding?

"Hi, Evan. I'm Alex," the man said, offering a regal smile.

"Hi, Evan," the teenage daughter acknowledged as well.

Evan flushed.

"So, uh, how much for these lights?" Tom asked, breaking up the pleasantries.

Alex fixed his gaze on Tom, studying him, but still smiling that regal smile. "We were thinking two dollars a strand. Unless, of course, you were trying to beat us this year for a shot at the Christmas Cup." He let out a chuckle at his own joke.

Tom tried to form his lips into a half-smile.

The daughter looked away, her attention caught on something at Tom's side.

"Trevor?" she asked.

Tom turned to see Trevor pop out from behind him.

Trevor looked up at the girl, but his face was cherry red, flushed with embarrassment.

"Your name's Trevor, right?"

"Yeah, it is," Trevor said in a low tone. "Kayla, was it?"

"Yeah," she exclaimed. "I think we are in the same math class."

"I think so."

Tom suddenly understood why Trevor had been acting so strange. He was embarrassed. Tom wasn't sure if it was because he was with his grandfather and brother and sister, or if it was because he was buying the used items that belonged to one of his classmates.

All attention returned to Tom when Kayla and Trevor's conversation came to a lull.

"How about fifty cents a strand?" Tom asked, breaking the silence.

"Grandpa!" Trevor whispered, just loud enough for Tom to hear, but not for Kayla or her father. Clearly, Tom was embarrassing Trevor even more.

Alex tilted his head as if studying Tom and his straightforward negotiation tactics.

"Oh, come on, Dad," Kayla said, pleading with him.

He looked down at her. "Oh, all right. Deal," Alex said. He reached across the table to offer Tom his hand.

The sucker didn't know that fifty cents had just been Tom's opening bid, but Tom wasn't going to let him in on it. He reached across and shook his hand. "Deal," Tom said while grabbing for his wallet. It was more money than he wanted to spend, but for under eighty bucks, Tom doubted he could get even a tenth of this many lights anywhere else.

"Hope you don't go beating us with those lights this year," Alex said while taking the money.

Tom shrugged and then reached down for a box. Trevor, Kayla, and Alex helped as well, and together they carried them out to the Bronco.

Tom led the way past the tables of stuff, then along the impeccable front yard of pristine green grass and rosebushes of every color imaginable. To keep a yard so colorful in winter obviously meant some serious time and money had gone into it. Only people trying to show off did stuff like that, and people like that annoyed Tom.

Suddenly, his right leg shot with pain, like a knife tearing its way out from the inside. Tom fell forward on impact and the box of lights went flying. He collided hard with the ground, using his hands to brace for impact as the lights scattered. His leg went completely numb, and for a split second, he wondered if he'd shattered it, but then the feeling came back, leaving a dull ache.

All three kids ran to him, shouting, "Grandpa!"

"Are you okay?" Alex called frantically, rushing to Tom's side.

"Yeah, yeah. I'm fine," he grumbled and pressed himself up. Blood rushed to his head while he struggled to lift himself.

Alex clutched his arm to help him.

"I said I'm fine," Tom snapped.

Alex let go, taken aback.

"It's the dang sidewalk. You're going to kill someone with that uneven pavement," Tom continued. He pointed back toward the pavement, but when everyone turned, he could see they'd each realized there was nothing uneven about it. The sidewalk was flawlessly flat.

"Sorry about that," Alex said.

Kayla rushed to grab the box, placing the miraculously unbroken lights back into it before handing it back.

"You sure you're okay, sir?" Alex continued, still not convinced. "That looked pretty bad."

"I'm fine." Tom grabbed the box from Kayla, then opened the trunk and set it inside. The others set their boxes inside as well.

Alex gave him a skeptical look before shrugging, and then he turned back around to return to the garage sale.

The kids climbed into the car, and Kayla waved to Trevor as Tom put the car into drive and drove off down the street, his leg still aching from the sudden burst of diabetic neuropathy.

A flock of birds flew by overhead, probably making its way south for the winter that was fast approaching. Tom and the kids had been in the garage for several hours, and they had lost track of time.

Evan and Brittany decided to take a break, opting for a game of hide-and-go-seek instead. Tom and Trevor continued working.

"This is so dumb. How much longer do we have to do this?" Trevor asked impatiently.

Tom looked up. "As long as it takes."

Trevor struggled to untangle yet another strand of lights, this one with large green bulbs. When he finally finished, he handed it to Tom for testing. Tom plugged it into the extension cord he'd set up, and the string of lights lit up. Well, some of it did. Two lights at the end were out, which had been the case for several of the strands they'd been through already.

"See, that one doesn't work either! Why can't we just buy some new ones?"

Tom unplugged the strand, then brought the bulbs that hadn't worked closer to his eyes. "I told you already, have patience, and we will get them to work."

Trevor scoffed.

Tom glanced over at the rat's nest of garbled lights Trevor was struggling to untangle. Laughing to himself, he started working on the string in front of him.

"Why can't *you* untangle while *I* test them then?" Trevor pushed further.

"Trevor, I told you already. I'm not just testing the lights, I'm fixing them. Do you want to work the wiring and change out the circuits?"

Trevor rolled his eyes and went back to untangling the mangled strand.

As an electrician, Tom had learned the ins and outs of working with shorted bulbs, bad circuits, and twisted wiring. Not to say that it was easy work; it often took several attempts before the fixes worked, but Tom didn't mind it. During all the years he'd entered the Christmas Cup Competition, Tom had never once thrown out a strand. Holly always insisted he just pick up a new one at the store to prevent the hours of work it sometimes took to fix the strands, but Tom was resilient. There wasn't a strand that he couldn't fix, so why waste money on new ones? It wasn't until two years ago, after the accident, that Tom had finally thrown a strand away. In fact, he'd thrown most of them away, with the exception of one box. Getting rid of the boxes had been therapeutic, but after several attempts, he hadn't been able to bring himself to throw out the box of lights from his and Holly's first Christmas together. Instead, he'd kept it hidden in the garage—until the kids had found it, of course.

Tom twisted out a bulb and checked the wiring for anything that might be loose, but couldn't find anything. He moved on to the next bulb. A moment later, Noel's minivan pulled into the driveway.

Evan leapt out from behind the cabinet.

"Found you!" Brittany called.

Brittany and Evan stood up and ran to the minivan as it came to a stop.

"Mommy!" Evan yelled. He jumped into her arms for a hug.

Brittany came up from behind to join in. Noel hugged them back then walked over to Trevor and tousled his hair. He grimaced.

"Were you guys good for Tom?" Noel asked.

Tom glanced up from the bulb in his hand. He saw Noel smiling from ear to ear, looking even happier than she had when she'd gotten the job.

"Yeah!" Evan shouted. "We helped Grandpa untangle and test the Christmas lights."

"Oh, you did, did you?" Noel asked.

"Yeah, but it's stupid," Trevor said. "We should just get new lights. We've had to fix every strand. We should be out there putting them up already."

"These strands work perfectly well," Tom said. "Just need to teach Trevor some patience is all."

Noel laughed.

"How was work, Mom?" Brittany asked.

"It was great, honey. I got to make coffee today, and the people there are so nice. Shall we head inside so I can make you some dinner?"

"Mac and cheese?" Evan asked.

"Mac and cheese," Noel agreed.

"Yay!"

The kids scooted off through the door and into the house while Tom continued to fidget with the strand. After two more bulbs, he finally found the loose wire. He glanced down at the box—still at least twenty more strands to go. Looked like he'd have to do it himself. Not like the kids were much help anyway, complaining every chance they could.

Noel appeared in the doorway.

"Hey, Tom," she said.

Tom looked up as he grabbed another tangled strand from the box.

"Thanks for watching the kids today. Sounds like they had fun. And thanks for agreeing to enter the Christmas Cup Competition. It really means a lot to them."

A lump formed in Tom's throat. Again, part of him wanted to be sympathetic and return to being the type of father he'd once been, but he reminded himself that it wasn't possible. "Yeah, yeah. Those kids need to learn patience. Otherwise I might have to reconsider entering this year."

Noel nodded and turned to start back toward the house.

Tom went back to the strand and began to shake it to try to loosen the knots, but the shaking only seemed to make them worse. He couldn't figure out for the life of him why the Garcettis hadn't just wrapped each strand into a circle like normal people do.

"This doggone string!" Tom rattled it harder, losing patience with every passing second. Soon, the strand was even more tangled than when he'd first started.

Noel laughed as she walked back inside. "Looks like the kids aren't the only ones who need a lesson in patience," she said under her breath.

CHAPTER 7

MONDAY, DECEMBER 7

The smell of fresh ground coffee graced Noel's nostrils as she walked through the door. Several patrons glanced up from their devices. She smiled at them as she walked by.

Behind the counter was a face she hadn't expected. Tate. His burly brown beard had been trimmed down slightly, and his hair was slicked perfectly to the side. He wore a navy-blue Henley, unbuttoned at the top to show off his well-defined chest. Noel reminded herself that she was here to work, not ogle. She'd seen what had happened when she'd finally opened herself up to men again with Bryan. Plus, Tate was a married man and her boss, no less.

"Good morning, Noel," he said, showing off his pearly white teeth in a smile.

"Morning, Tate," Noel answered pleasantly. "I didn't expect to see you here today." She made her way around the counter before setting down her purse under the counter and grabbing for a brown apron.

"Do I sense disappointment?" Tate asked.

"No, no, of course not." Noel laughed nervously. "Just didn't know how often you worked since I didn't see you over the weekend during my training."

"Oh, so you're saying I don't work enough." Tate's eyebrows furrowed, all of a sudden looking visibly upset. "I'm just one of those owners that comes in to cash my checks. That it?"

Noel's eyes flashed to his, realizing the hole she'd just dug herself into. "No, Tate, I'm sorry—" she stammered.

Tate burst into laughter.

Noel stared at him, unsure what was happening.

"Noel, I'm kidding. Just giving you a hard time."

It took a second before she loosened up enough to let out a nervous chuckle. Tate put a hand on her shoulder reassuringly.

"Sorry. Bad boss jokes, I know. So how were your first shifts? Anyone I need to beat up?"

Noel met his gaze as she washed her hands. "Of course not. They were great. Everyone is so nice. I really like it here."

Tate nodded. "Great. Sorry I couldn't make it in over the weekend. Had some . . . *stuff* I had to take care of."

He continued talking as he reached for a dish towel. "I usually try to work Monday through Friday anyway. I help out in the front when needed but mostly take care of the accounting and inventory in the back."

"Oh, so you get to do the fun stuff?" she teased.

Tate laughed again. "You have no idea."

Noel made her way to the counter beside him. "Okay, I'm ready to take over if you need to head on back." She straightened the pile of coffee cups in front of her.

Tate looked up from the mug he was drying. "You think you can handle it on your own?"

"I think I can handle it. Josephine taught me well. Plus, the drink list is right here if I get stuck." Noel gestured toward a laminated recipe sheet to the right of a bag of Columbian roast.

Tate set down the towel and smiled. "Okay. I'll be in the back if they start to bite."

Noel laughed again and then started working. Tate disappeared into the back.

For the first time in her life, she was getting paid for what she did. It felt good, and she enjoyed it. Most of the customers seemed to be regulars, and Noel was already trying to get each of their names down. She'd learned from Josephine, the twenty-year-old college student, that Tate had opened up a year and a half ago after moving to town. Josephine swore he was the best boss she'd ever had, but offered little in the way of details about the man. Besides the fact that he owned the place, seemed great with people, and had moved to town a year and a half earlier, Noel didn't know much else about Tate. And something inside her longed to discover his story. Noel knew that habit came from her mother.

Holly had always been nosy, but not in an annoying way. She was great with people, and whenever there was something she wanted to find out, she made nice with whomever she had to until they became friends and eventually spilled the beans about whatever it was she wanted to know. Noel had seen her do that time and time again. Whether it was a secret family recipe a neighbor had or rumors of a new measure the city council was looking to pass, Holly always got what she wanted.

Noel continued to brew coffees and teas as customers came and went. She realized fairly quickly that the gingerbread latte was the most popular menu item with Christmas right around the corner. Noel fumbled with some of the drink orders, usually the ones who asked for soy instead of milk, or triple shots instead of single. But slowly and surely, she was getting the hang of it, and to her surprise, the tip jar began to fill up.

She hadn't actually seen a paycheck yet, but Josephine had insisted on sharing the tip money from Noel's training shifts. Noel had protested, being in training and all, but Josephine wouldn't have it. In two days, Noel ended up with sixty-eight dollars in tips. She certainly had much more to go if she wanted to find an apartment by December 24, but it was a start.

Money had always been one of the things she'd taken for granted. Jacob had handled the finances for years, and when it came time to pay rent, buy groceries, or shop for Christmas, she never had to worry. When she'd moved from place to place after his death, trying to find their perfect fresh start, she'd at least had the life insurance money. And then when that got close to its end, there was her relationship with Bryan, the construction worker. She'd met him at church one Sunday, and they immediately hit it off. One thing led to another, and soon he was offered a job in Sacramento. He'd let Noel and the kids move into his two-bedroom apartment after they got married and had always made sure food was on the table, but he didn't exactly make a lot of money.

Trevor had insisted that he thought Bryan was okay, but then again she always wondered if Trevor had only said that because he knew how much Noel had needed Bryan at the time. Even still, Noel had really thought things were going to work. Bryan reminded her of Jacob in so many ways. His swimmer's body, the brown hair, the construction job, even the sense of humor. When Noel and Bryan had been alone, things were good. Conversation was effortless, as were their interests in movies, TV, and music. Most of all, he made her smile again.

But the kids were young and expensive. After Bryan had proposed in front of the Golden Gate Bridge on a day trip to San Francisco, he'd started picking up extra shifts to cover the bills, and he'd also started coming home drunk. The first few times, he insisted it had just been a beer with the guys. But soon it became a recurring theme. When Noel insisted he join them for dinner, he'd lock himself in the bedroom. Any time the kids would try to ask him a question, he'd go quiet.

One day when he arrived home, he was drunk again, and this time he wasn't quiet. Instead, he was upset. He went off about how much Noel and the kids took him for granted, about how Trevor didn't respect him, and about how he could never replace their father. He told her she needed to move out, that he was filing for a divorce. That night, she'd pled for him to let her stay. But deep down, she knew he was right. The next morning, after calling every possible friend she'd thought she had, she'd called Tom. A week later, she packed the kids in the minivan then started to drive.

Now here she was, working in a coffee shop back in her hometown of Glenn Hills, California, living with her grumpy and aloof father. Life certainly wasn't perfect, but for the first time in a long time, things felt like they were on the way up.

"Kim, your frozen hot chocolate is ready," Noel called. She finished it off with whipped cream on top, then she slid it across the counter for a girl in a gray beanie to take.

The girl smiled, slipping a dollar into the tip jar and then taking a drink of her hot chocolate.

"Thanks so much! Enjoy," Noel said as she began to wipe down the counter.

The door opened and Noel turned to face her next customers. She smiled up at them as they walked in.

Four women dressed in nice designer clothes and dresses took off their sunglasses in unison.

"Did you see what she was wearing?" one of them snickered.

The rest laughed.

"Wait, that's not Tate," another said, a blonde with a short pixie cut and stilettos that made her look at least six feet tall.

"Yeah, I came to see that gorgeous hunk of man meat, Tate. Not this woman," another one added. She was a pretty, exotic-looking woman with sharp cheekbones and a lot of makeup, and for a second, Noel thought she recognized her.

"Sorry to disappoint," Noel interrupted. "I'm the new barista, Noel."

The women gave her a skeptical look, obvious disappointment splashed across their faces.

"Large caramel macchiato. Non-fat milk, one spoonful of honey, and extra whipped cream," the blonde one demanded.

"Peppermint chai with rice milk instead of regular. No whip. No cinnamon," another one, with wavy brunette hair and an expensive-looking pearl necklace, added.

"And a black coffee for me. Extra hot," a woman with bright pink lips and gold hoop earrings spoke as she looked down at her phone.

Noel rushed to jot each order on her pad, but they were talking at her too fast. She couldn't help but notice the way they talked down to her, no please or thanks mentioned by any of them. But the one thing she knew was the customer was always right, so she kept on smiling while taking down their orders.

"And I'll have a soy latte with a dash of honey and sprinkle of sugar," the pretty, exotic-looking one added.

Noel nodded as she finished writing it down. "Okay, great. Will you be paying together or separate?" she asked.

The exotic-looking one dug into her purse while the others struck up conversation at the exact same moment. "Just put it on my card," she said, lazily holding it out for Noel to take.

Noel punched the orders into the tablet. "Great. That will be sixteen dollars and sixty-two cents." The woman didn't acknowledge her and instead turned her back to Noel to face her friends. "Did you want to donate to the Christmas Cup Competition this year?" Noel added. It was something Josephine had told her to do, and to her surprise, most people complied. Maybe it was just that the customers of Glenn Hills Classic Coffee were nice, or maybe it was that people were more giving during the holiday season. Maybe it was both, but whatever it was, Noel liked it.

The women went silent, then each stared at Noel as though she'd just made crude remarks about each of their mothers.

"Do you know who this is?" the blonde one asked, gesturing to the woman paying.

"I apologize. I don't yet."

"This is Samantha Garcetti, as in the Garcetti family that's won the Christmas Cup Competition for the last five years straight."

The pretty, exotic woman flashed a smile, as though she were posing for the camera.

"Oh, I'm sorry. I'm just supposed to ask everyone if they'd like to donate." Noel didn't know whether to feel embarrassed or offended. She didn't quite see why it mattered if Samantha was the winner of the competition in the past or not. Probably even better that she pay it forward for the competition this year anyway.

"No problem. Why don't you put me down for a fifty-dollar donation toward the Cup," Samantha said.

"Okay, great. Really nice of you," Noel said. "My father and kids are entering the competition this year too. Maybe they'll give you a run for your money."

"Oh, that's nice. Tell them good luck for me," Samantha said, and the other women snickered.

Noel turned the tablet around for the woman to sign and add a tip. Samantha lazily touched her finger against it and a second later turned it back. The women continued their conversations and turned their backs to Noel. When Noel looked at the tablet before starting their drink orders, she noticed the dollar tip Samantha Garcetti had left. A dollar wasn't much compared to the drink total and donation, but it was at least something, and it was certainly more than she'd expected from the woman.

She began to work on the drinks, checking the ingredient list as she went. After some blending, frapping, mixing, and stirring, she finished. She looked up at the women to let them know their drinks were ready when she noticed the one who'd paid, Samantha Garcetti, watching her.

Noel offered a polite smile and then slid the drinks across the counter after double checking each one.

"Wait, did you say your name is Noel?" Samantha asked inquisitively.

All three of her friends stopped conversing and looked up as well.

"Yes," Noel said.

"Noel VanHansen?"

"Yes. How'd you know that?"

"Oh my gosh. We used to go to high school together. Didn't you date Jacob Hunt?"

Suddenly, realization settled in. The overly made-up face. The taste for high fashion. The better-than-you attitude. Samantha Garcetti was Samantha Alvarez from high school. As in the Samantha and Alice that'd bullied her and called her "Quiet VanHansen." As in the Samantha and Alice who'd tried to stop Jacob from talking to her and who'd tried to steal a dance at prom.

"Oh, Samantha. Yes, I think I remember you. Yeah, Jacob and I got married."

"Wow, look who grew up. Congrats. I don't think I've seen you back in Glenn Hills since high school. So what are you up to these days? You must be all successful now that you married the high school hunk. Wait." She paused for a moment to exchange a look with the women. "Do you own Glenn Hills Classic Coffee? We love this place."

Noel knew enough to recognize when someone was being nice and when someone was trying to embarrass her. It was clear by the apron and from the fact that the women knew Tate that Noel was, in fact, not the owner, but rather just a worker. No, this was Samantha's way of making herself feel good about herself at Noel's expense.

"No, actually, I just moved back to town and I'm working here part-time. And actually Jacob passed away, and now I'm simply trying to take care of my three kids."

Samantha took a moment before replying, clearly trying to measure her words without coming off as a blatant jerk. There was a softness in her eyes. "Wow. That is so admirable of you. I'm sure it isn't easy taking a job like *this*."

Noel didn't take the bait. She kept the smile on her face and gestured toward the drinks. "Well, enjoy your coffees. Good to see you again, Samantha."

The women took their drinks and went on their way. As soon as they got through the door, however, she could see them practically burst into conversation, each of them looking back at Noel through the window.

Noel knew she shouldn't be upset with them. She knew that Samantha was just a lonely bully who had to buy her friends' drinks in order to get them to hang out with her, but it still hurt. The way she'd acted as though Noel had become a second-class citizen by taking a part-time, entry-level job. Flaunting her money and fame from winning the Christmas Cup Competition. Noel knew that Samantha was a bully, just like she always had been.

Noel tried to brush it off and put on a smile when Tate stepped out of the doorway to the back office and called out to her.

"You okay?" he asked, his voice sympathetic and low.

"Me? I'm fine," she said, pretending nothing had happened.

"I only heard the end of your conversation with those women, but I have to say, you handled it like a champ. They left before I could say something. I would have kicked them out."

Noel looked up. "Really? But you'd lose business. And they'd talk."

"So? My shop. My rules. No jerks allowed."

Noel laughed when Tate gave her a half-smile.

Silence hung in the air afterward as Tate moved toward the sink to wash his hands and put on an apron.

"Why don't I join you out here for a bit?" he said.

Noel nodded and went to the counter to wipe down a dash of cinnamon she'd spilled while making the drinks.

"I overheard what you said about your husband. I'm sorry."

Noel turned around to see the rugged man offering her what seemed to be a sincere look of sympathy. He didn't look to be the type of guy that got sentimental, but as Holly had always told her, don't judge a book by its cover. "Thanks. It was five years ago. I'm all right now." Noel started to look away, but then Tate touched her arm softly.

"Still, it isn't easy."

Noel smiled at him softly in response.

He nodded and let go. "Don't listen to what those women have to say. Maybe I'm biased, but I think you are better off than them."

"You do, do you?" Noel asked.

"Yeah, I mean for starters you have a cool boss," Tate said. "Plus, you are a hard worker and friendly with people. We might not be able to say the same for those women. Plus you are an exceptional mother."

"The cool boss part is certainly arguable," Noel teased, bringing a laugh out of Tate. "And who's to say I'm a good mom anymore? Sure doesn't feel like it these days. My oldest son barely talks to me anymore. And because I kept looking for a fresh start, I've made them switch schools three times in the past five years." When she looked up, she found Tate smirking and realized she'd taken the moment too far with her new boss. "Sorry, too personal. I know you were just trying to cheer me up. Thank you."

Tate paused from cleaning the counter. "Noel, it wasn't too personal. If you ever need to talk, my door's always open. Figuratively, of course. We do close the shop. But seriously, I'm here if you need me."

Noel smiled and nodded. Again, it felt like there was a connection between them, and she wanted to ask him more about himself, but she reminded herself that she needed to remember what had happened with the last man she'd felt a connection with.

She turned back to the door, looking for a distraction. A moment later, a couple wearing matching white scarves came inside, providing what she needed.

CHAPTER 8

TUESDAY, DECEMBER 8

The moment Tom had been looking forward to all week had finally arrived: Tuesday morning waffles at Bertha's Diner. But as much as he had been looking forward to it, Tom could tell things were not going as he had hoped.

"The Little Drummer Boy" hummed in the background, toying with Tom's already unusually high stress levels from the past week. Add in the fact that his usual view of downtown Glenn Hills was obstructed by the snowflake mural the teenage kid had painted last week, and this had the makings of a very annoying day.

"Will you hurry up with that syrup, Putz?" Tom demanded.

Richard looked up with a wide grin, then he purposefully tilted the syrup up slightly so it took even longer to pour out. "Wait your turn, Turbo."

Tom scowled and turned his attention to the hot plate of golden waffles in front of him.

"Hey, you two," Bertha warned as she refilled their mugs with hot coffee. "I might actually have to ban you from this place if you can't behave."

"We both know you wouldn't know what to do with yourself if you didn't get to see my beautiful face," Richard returned.

Bertha stuck out her tongue and then moved on to the next table.

"You think she likes me?" Richard slid the syrup across the table.

Tom wasted no time pouring it all over his plate of waffles. "You ask me that every week. Every week my answer is the same." He set the syrup down, then he cut into the waffle with his fork. "She doesn't like you. Do you really think you could ever replace Marlene?"

Richard looked up, his eyes wide. "Of course not, it's just a joke. I thought that's what you and I did? Normally this is when you make some sort of remark about how ugly, wrinkled, and slow I am. Then we go back to eating waffles and reading our newspapers."

"Well, you are ugly, wrinkled, and slow," Tom said, giving him a half-smile.

Richard laughed, took a long sip of his coffee, and then turned back to meet Tom's eyes. "Speaking of Marlene, you get back to treatment last week?"

It was the question Tom had been dreading. "No, I didn't. All the doctor is going to tell me is to eat better and get in more walking. Plus, what's Marlene have to do with it? She died of a heart attack, not diabetes."

Richard set down his mug. "Marlene died of a heart attack that stemmed from diabetes. The same disease you have. Now don't be stupid. You want to end up like that?"

Tom grunted something indiscernible under his breath. He'd known this wasn't going to be a good day the second he'd walked in. The Christmas music, the Christmas window display, the gray clouds outside. And now Richard wanted to get all serious. Tom knew he shouldn't have brought up Marlene like that, but something inside had flipped the second Tom had thought about trying to move on from Holly, just as Richard had joked about with Marlene.

He shoved another bite of waffles into his mouth, trying to move on from the conversation, but Richard wasn't having it.

"Have you told Noel about the treatments yet?"

"What's Noel got to do with it? The treatment is just another excuse for the doctor to get more money. I'm fine. It's just a bunch of gibberish nonsense."

"Really? Gibberish nonsense? Why don't you tell that to Marlene? Or Holly for that matter." Richard was getting loud now. This wasn't the Richard that Tom normally saw. Tom had seen glimpses three years back when Marlene had died, but the depressed, angry, and serious Richard, grieving with his loss, had soon gone right back to the sarcastic, jokey, and witty Richard that Glenn Hills had come to know and love.

"Okay, which of you two is getting kicked out?" Bertha interrupted, setting another pitcher of syrup on the table.

Both Tom and Richard stayed silent.

"Wow, you two really are fighting like a husband and wife," she added, then she turned to walk back to the kitchen.

Tom picked up his copy of the *Glenn Hills Times* and began to scan through it, looking for a distraction from the conversation. A moment later, Richard grabbed his copy too. But before Tom had read more than halfway down the page, he realized the prevailing news of the day was pertaining to the Christmas Cup Competition. An article about the early preparations. Another article about a new round of judges, several of them business owners rather than city council members. Tom scanned the names and came across Tate Roberts, the owner of Glenn Hills Classic Coffee. Wasn't that the place where Noel said she worked now? Tom wondered if the tides may actually be in his favor this year. Granted, his house was beat up and falling apart on the outside, and he didn't have one of those high-tech music-light-show displays, but Tom did have a plan.

"Looks like the city is going to impose a water tax next month," Richard said without looking away from the paper. "Just another way they can get more money out of working men like you and me."

"Hmm. Those money-sucking scoundrels always find a way to shake us down, don't they?" Tom turned the page to find the article Richard had mentioned, and finally the tension from their more serious conversation about health and treatments was over. It was back to their usual moaning and groaning about local politics.

They finished their waffles and coffees, and they went their separate ways.

Richard waved while backing out of his parking spot, and instead of backing out at the same time, Tom waited until Richard drove off. Then he exited his car and walked down the sidewalk to Glenn Hills Classic Coffee.

When he reached the window, he peered inside. Several young hippie-looking kids sat at tables looking at phones and laptops, many of them sitting across from each other, but no one conversing. Long gone were the times when you could just sit down and talk. Now everyone had to communicate through text message or whatever other fancy methods there were these days.

Tom spotted Noel a moment later, smiling behind the counter while handing a woman a mug. Noel said something Tom couldn't hear, and the woman put a dollar into the tip jar. Something about the scene saddened Tom. His own daughter having to work this kind of job. Tom was raised in a time when men were the ones to provide for their women. It was a shame what had happened with Jacob, and at that moment, Tom wished there was more he could do for his daughter, even if she hated his guts.

He scanned the coffee shop for any other workers, but it appeared she was alone. No Tate Roberts in sight. Tom would have to let Noel know later that the store owner was one of the judges, and if she could, she should try to make nice on his behalf.

"Mom, can I help Grandpa with the Christmas lights?" Evan shouted from the back seat.

"After your homework, honey."

Evan grumbled his disapproval.

"Can I help too, Mom?" Trevor asked.

Noel glanced over to the passenger seat in surprise. Trevor was volunteering to help Tom? Was this some sort of alternate universe? "Do you have homework?"

"Nope."

Noel gave him a skeptical look.

"I swear."

"Okay, as long as Grandpa is okay with it."

"Me too, Mom!" Brittany added from the back seat.

Noel laughed. Tom had no idea what was coming for him.

The kids darted through the back gate to look for Tom, but he wasn't sitting in the recliner as he normally was. After a bit of extra searching, they found him in the garage, working on the strands of lights.

"What's the matter?" Tom demanded.

"Can we help?" Evan asked.

"Evan, homework," Noel interrupted.

Evan shrugged and stomped off through the door leading into the house. Brittany followed.

"Can I help?" Trevor asked.

Tom looked up. "I suppose. Just about ready to start putting them up outside." He lifted a strand from the box and handed it to Trevor.

"I'll let you two be. I'm going to get dinner started," Noel said before walking back into the house.

Trevor and Tom getting along? Tom entering the Christmas Cup Competition? Brittany and Evan excited about a new school and enjoying living with Tom? What the heck was happening here?

When Bryan kicked them out, she thought things could only get worse driving home to stay with Tom. Strangely, the kids seemed happier than they had been living in Sacramento. Even Tom was more pleasant than she'd expected, to the extent you could call his behavior congenial, at least. Now she even had a job. A real job that she genuinely liked and was earning her actual money.

Today at work she hadn't had any more run-ins with Samantha and her posse. It also seemed that she actually had a good boss. Tate was nothing like the stories she'd heard of people hating their boss's guts. They'd had more time to talk today about their favorite coffees, and he'd even asked about her kids. Work was good, and her kids were good, but what about her? As hard as it was without a man in her life, she felt somewhat free. No man to cook and clean for. No man to worry about whether she or her kids would offend. Sure, she missed the conversations, date nights, and intimacy, but not as much as she thought she would. Not yet at least.

Noel glanced outside the kitchen window as Tom stomped across the barren lawn with Trevor following behind, Christmas lights in hand, and she felt her lips begin to curl upward into a grin.

CHAPTER 9

Doggone Christmas lights. Get them to work one minute, and they go out the next.

Tom struggled to unhook yet another strand from the eaves after seeing that it had gone out. Probably another busted fuse. That would make eight so far.

"Would you look at that?" an old voice croaked from behind him. "My eyes must be deceiving me."

Tom turned to find Richard holding Christie's leash on the sidewalk. "Mind your own business, Richard."

Tom turned back to the task at hand, but he knew Richard wouldn't leave that easily.

"You aren't trying for the Cup again, are you?" Richard asked, trudging through the lawn toward him as Tom tried his best to act busy. "You must have seen that article about the winnings reaching upwards of fifteen thousand dollars because I can't think of any other reason Scrooge himself would be celebrating Christmas."

"Would you quit your yapping, Richard? Just because I put up the dang lights doesn't mean I'm celebrating Christmas," Tom snapped, fiddling with the fuse between his calloused fingers.

"There's the Tom I know," Richard said. "For a second there I thought you might have gone soft."

"No one can be as soft as you and that belly of yours, Putz."

Silence hung in the air while Tom continued to work the lights.

"You get back to treatment this morning?" Richard asked softly.

"Again, none of your business," Tom said. "But if you must know, no, I didn't. Noel needed me to get the kids ready for school. Plus, I'm fine."

"Don't you think you should tell Noel? She is staying with you, after all. What if something happens?"

"Richard," Tom warned, "I'll tell her on my own time, thank you very much." He glared at Richard, and after a moment, Richard gave in and shrugged.

Christie barked, her tongue hanging out of her mouth while looking up to Tom for attention.

"Yeah, yeah," Tom said. He set down the strand of lights and reached down to pet Christie.

Christie's curly white tail began to wag from side to side.

"Grandpa!" Evan yelled.

He darted from the side of the house toward them. *Looks like school's out.* Brittany followed behind. At the back of the pack, Trevor walked slowly across the yard, spiky hair and black clothes as always.

As soon as Evan saw the little fluffy white dog, his attention flipped a switch. "Is this our Christmas present?" he screamed.

"Mom got us a dog?" Brittany asked, full of enthusiasm.

Richard laughed. "Sorry to be the bearer of bad news, but Christie is my dog."

"Aw, man," Evan sulked.

Brittany's smile diminished too.

Trevor approached, but stayed silent in the background.

"Do you want to pet her?" Richard offered.

Evan looked up at the thin, balding, old man and nodded.

Richard smiled. "Go right on ahead then."

Evan knelt down so that he was at eye level with Christie, then he reached his hand to her back. Slowly, he began to pet her. Christie's tail wagged and she opened her mouth in what appeared to be a smile. Brittany reached down to pet her too, and the next second, Christie rolled onto her back. Evan and Brittany laughed as they began to rub her belly. Christie kicked her legs with joy while her tongue stuck out of the side of her mouth. Even Tom let out a little laugh at the scene.

"What's going on here?" Noel called, now approaching from behind the house too. She smiled when she noticed Richard with them. "Oh, hi, Richard!"

"Noel, so good to see you. Hope you don't mind if the kids pet Christie."

"No, of course not. Anything to keep them occupied." She smiled as she looked down at the scene, the kids laughing as they rubbed Christie's belly, and Christie enjoying every second of the attention. "It's been a while since I've seen you last. How are things?"

"Oh, can't complain. Sometimes a bit lonely without Marlene, but I have your dad for company. And Christie and I stay pretty busy with all the walks. She really tires me out most days."

Noel offered a polite smile.

"Who's Marlene?" Evan asked.

Richard's expression softened. "Marlene was my wife. She passed away not long ago. She had a heart attack." His eyes fixed on Tom.

Tom got the message, loud and clear.

"Why don't we let Richard get back to walking Christie?" Tom said, hoping to end the conversation.

Christie rolled back onto her feet after Brittany and Evan stopped petting her.

"Mom, can we get a dog like Christie for Christmas?" Brittany asked.

This was turning out to be a far worse conversation than Tom could have anticipated. Tom knew that neither Noel nor himself would be able to afford a dog, and that wasn't a question Tom wanted to be the one to answer.

"I don't think so, sweetie. Dogs are a lot of work and can be expensive."

Brittany's face sank in defeat. Evan's did too.

"I have an idea. If it's okay with your mom, that is," Richard interrupted. "Would you two be interested in walking Christie for me? She tires me out, and I could pay you a couple of bucks each walk."

Tom looked to Noel, who was clearly contemplating it.

"What do you think guys?" she asked.

Glee radiated from Evan's face. "Can we?"

"Yeah, can we, Mom?" Brittany demanded.

"Oh, all right."

"Yay!" they shouted in unison.

"Okay, great. Why don't I go with you two this time so that I can show you what to do?" Richard said while looking down at the kids.

"Thanks, Richard," Noel said. "I'm going to get dinner started inside. Why don't you join us for dinner, Richard?"

"Oh, that's kind of you, but I have leftovers that aren't going to take care of themselves. Thank you, though. Rain check," Richard replied.

Noel smiled and nodded, then turned to Tom. "You two okay out here?" She looked from Tom to Trevor. They both nodded. "Okay, have fun," she said. Then she headed back to the house, waving good-bye to Richard and the kids.

"I'll have them back in a couple days," Richard teased as he, Christie, Evan, and Brittany left for their walk.

Tom picked up the strand of lights he'd been working on before Richard's interruption.

"What can I do to help?" Trevor asked shyly.

Tom glanced over at the spiky-haired kid, somewhat caught off guard. "You know how to work a staple gun?"

Trevor nodded. "Yeah. Bryan showed me last year, working on our apartment. Well, our old apartment."

Unsure of what to say, Tom grabbed the staple gun off the lawn and handed it to Trevor. "Why don't you climb up on the ladder and start stapling the lights in place every couple of feet?"

Once Trevor was on the ladder working, Tom couldn't help noticing that Trevor was taller than he'd realized. Probably getting close to six feet already.

Tom replaced a fuse while Trevor made quick work along the eaves.

Trevor became stuck when one of the sections he tried to staple into broke open on impact. Termite damage. Yet another thing Tom needed to fix on the outdated house.

He joined Trevor after replacing the fuses and began to hand him the strands as he went along. The silence between them felt heavy. Tom wasn't much for talking, but he also wasn't one for awkward silences.

"So," Tom started while Trevor kept going at the eaves, "how you liking your new school?"

Trevor glanced down. "It's okay."

Short and direct. Tom wondered ruefully where he got it from. "Classes hard?"

"Nope. The classwork is easy."

Tom had seen Trevor's schedule on the table the other morning. The boy had been signed up for every advanced class known to man. Must have inherited the brains from his mother—and grandmother, for that matter. Holly had always been smarter than Tom, and there was no denying it. Finances, taxes, Jeopardy trivia, and just about anything else that required a bit of brains all came from her.

"Meet any friends?"

"Not really," Trevor said.

Tom studied him. His grandson wasn't an easy nut to crack.

"What about that girl from the garage sale. What was her name?"

"Who? Kayla?" Trevor asked quickly.

Tom noticed the slight flush in his face as he said it. "Yeah. Kayla. You talk to her?"

"A little. Just in class. She's nice."

Tom wasn't good at this type of small talk, but he could tell that Trevor liked this girl. Trevor was a boy of few words, but Tom could see it in his eyes. He had a crush.

They kept at the Christmas lights, Tom directing Trevor as they went.

A few minutes passed when finally, Trevor broke the silence. "How'd you meet Grandma?"

Tom stopped. It hadn't been a question he had expected, nor was it one he wanted to answer. People didn't ask him questions about Holly because they knew it wasn't the sort of thing to ask a grieving man like Tom. "Uh, I'd prefer if we didn't talk about your grandmother."

Trevor nodded. "Oh, okay. Sorry." He picked the strand back up and held it against the eave for another staple.

Tom sighed, registering Trevor's disappointment instantly. This was the first real chance he had at developing something with his grandson, and he was throwing it away. "We met in high school. Freshman year."

Trevor looked down at Tom, surprised. "High school? I didn't know that."

Tom hesitated, weighing whether or not to continue. Every memory he carried of Holly, the woman he'd created a life with, was difficult, but the stories of how they first met were the hardest. "We sat next to each other in English. She was smarter than me, so I usually tried to cheat off her work. Most of the time she wouldn't let me."

Trevor's jaw dropped. "You cheated?"

"Yeah, I wasn't as smart as you or your mother. You inherited your brains from your grandmother."

Trevor let out a laugh, then put another staple into the eave.

Tom continued. "Well, one day Holly noticed me looking over at her paper. When Holly told me to stop, our teacher, Ms. Smith, came over to us. She took both of our papers and sent us to detention."

Trevor stopped what he was doing and looked down from the ladder, an expression of astonishment splashed across his face. "You got detention?"

"Yup. And so did Holly. Well, Holly hadn't ever had a detention, but I'd certainly had my fair share. Actually, one more strike and I was due for a suspension."

Tom fiddled with the fuse in his fingers and looked down, remembering the story as though it were yesterday.

He continued. "Holly told me she would tell the principal and my mom what really happened. And that's exactly what she did."

"What did they do?" Trevor asked while moving the ladder over.

"I got suspended. But she got in trouble too. The principal called it a lesson in 'helping' others. Ended up making her tutor me once a week in English. Boy, was she upset. At first, she refused, but when the principal threatened another detention, she gave in."

Trevor laughed and looked down after climbing the ladder again. "You got suspended?"

"Yup. And my mom gave me the belt. I don't think it actually hurt, but it was the humiliation that was worse than anything else. Soon, Holly started coming over to tutor me."

Trevor laughed some more, and Tom couldn't help but join in. "Did it help?" Trevor asked.

"Not at first. I was distracted by her. Prettiest girl in the whole school with her blonde hair and sundresses. I couldn't focus. And she made me nervous. My grade in the class didn't get any better, which meant she was failing as a tutor, and she didn't like failing, so one day she really grabbed my attention. She told me if I got an A on my next test, she would take me on a date. And, boy, let me tell you, it worked. I studied like there was no tomorrow and got an A. I don't think she expected me to, though, because when I showed her the test, all she said was 'good job.' I had to ask her about the deal before she finally acted as though she remembered."

Tom smiled to himself while remembering how taken aback Holly had been. Trevor put in another staple. "So what did you do then?"

"Hi, Grandpa!" Evan shouted from across the lawn.

Trevor and Tom glanced toward the interruption. Richard, Brittany, Evan, and Christie stood at the brick wall between Tom's and Richard's houses.

"Christie really likes these two whippersnappers," Richard called.

Christie wagged her tail while Evan and Brittany ran across the lawn.

"I want a dog like Christie, Grandpa," Brittany said.

Tom waved to Richard who gave him a wink before turning back to his house. What was the wink for?

"Kids, dinner's ready," Noel called through the window.

Evan and Brittany ran toward the back gate at the announcement.

Trevor stayed put on the ladder. "So what happened next?" Trevor finally asked now that they were alone.

"Trevor, come on," Noel shouted.

Tom glanced over to the window. "You better get inside. We'll continue that story another time."

Trevor simply nodded. He climbed down the ladder, set down the lights, and then walked to the back gate. He glanced once more at Tom. Then he went inside.

CHAPTER 10

You want something done, you do it yourself.

As much as Tom didn't want to admit it, having Trevor around to help untangle and put up lights had made things go faster. The ladders may have been easy back in his electrician days, but the darn things felt more and more unstable as time went on. Tom wasn't sure if ladders were made better back then, or if somehow his balance had been thrown off over the years. He didn't much care for the second possibility, so he concluded it had to be the first. Either way, Trevor was at school for the day, and Tom didn't want to wait around. The Christmas Cup Competition was underway, and if he wanted a shot at winning and collecting the money, he needed to get to it.

That day, Tom decided to forgo his morning western movie marathon and his afternoon nap, adding to his growing tiredness which, in turn, added to his growing annoyance. But slowly and surely, his plan was coming to life.

In the afternoon, he stopped to observe his work.

Tom had managed to use one light for every foot of the house. Each strand started from the bottom, then went straight up the house until it reached the top, from which the strand would move to the left one foot, and start in a line straight back down the house. Tom had also wrapped all three of the tall oak trees from top to bottom. At least as far as the ladder would allow. All the bushes were wrapped in a similar manner, covering every square foot. The only area left was the roof, and Tom decided he'd save that for Trevor. Trevor had shown a genuine interest in exterior illumination, and Tom had a feeling the boy wouldn't want to be left out. Also, Tom didn't feel the risk of being on the roof was worth it for a man of his age, but he wasn't going to admit that to anyone else.

Once Trevor finished the roof, every foot of the house would be covered. That was exactly how Tom wanted it; that way all eyes were drawn toward the lights and away from the dead front lawn, faded paint, and outdated roof shingles. Tom still had a bit of finagling to do in order to ensure another part of his plan would work; he was going to put the circuits on timers. If his neighbors could time their lights to music, Tom could certainly time his to make a show of it.

But that wasn't even the best part.

The beauty was that the best part was simple, and he knew people would love it. It was a cheap trick, but that didn't matter because all he needed was for people to see it, love it, and talk about it. He wanted to win this thing once and for all.

Finally, after Tom had spent an entire day hanging lights, Noel's minivan pulled into the driveway. She must have finished work early enough to pick the kids up.

Brittany and Evan jetted out of the minivan and across the lawn.

"Hi, Grandpa," they called together. He'd expected them to stop and hug his waist, but the next second they shot by him and continued on.

Tom watched as the kids made their way to Richard's. *Oh yeah, dog walking.* He wasn't so sure that it was a good idea. The kids would likely get attached, and soon enough they'd be moving out. Even worse, he knew they'd beg Noel for a dog of their own, but that wasn't his problem to deal with. Tom stood from the wiring he was working with against the wall when Noel called out to him.

"Trevor has some homework to finish. I told him he can come help once he's done."

"Okay," Tom muttered, moving back toward the wall.

"I just wanted to say thank you for doing this. The kids love it, and it really means a lot," Noel said, walking toward him from the minivan.

Tom mumbled something indiscernible while turning back to the wires, but then he remembered something. "Hey, your boss is that Tate Roberts fellow, right?"

Noel tilted her head at the question. "Yeah, he's been really nice. Worked with him today actually. Why?"

"He's one of the Christmas Cup Competition judges this year. I just thought it might be worth mentioning. You know, for the kids?"

Noel seemed to already understand what he was getting at, her expression looking skeptical now. "I thought you were just doing this to help make them feel special?"

"I am," Tom said. "But it would make them feel more special if they won, don't you think?"

Noel shook her head. She looked like she was about to say something, but instead she decided to bite her tongue. She turned and walked back across the lawn.

Tom went back to work on the house, and a moment later he heard laughing from behind him. He turned to see Brittany and Evan walking Christie, with Richard by their side.

"Can't wait to see the lights all lit up," Richard said while strolling by. "But you better watch out. Competition's gonna be fierce this year. I was thinking I'd throw my hat in the ring too."

Tom lifted a hand to the air to brush Richard off. "Good luck figuring out how to plug them in. We all remember what happened last time."

"Sounds like there's some fear in your voice."

Tom looked down, trying to suppress a grin, then he got back to work as Richard and the kids walked on by. He wondered if Richard was really going to try, or if he was just giving Tom a hard time. The last time Richard had tried, he'd blown a circuit by overloading it. He'd plugged in nearly fifteen strands of lights on one circuit. Anyone who knew anything about electricity knew that six to eight strands was typically the max. Richard had ended up blowing the power for the entire street. Even if Richard did decide to throw his hat in, Tom wasn't the least bit worried.

Trevor came out shortly after, and Tom made quick work of getting him onto the roof.

To Tom's surprise, Trevor seemed perfectly at home on top of the roof. Tom told him to stay careful, then he got to work on the last part of the display. Bad grandparenting? Maybe, but the boy had to learn hard work at some point in his life. Tom sure had, and it had turned him into the man he was today.

"Come on, Mom!" Trevor yelled.

It was the moment they'd all been waiting for, the big reveal.

Most of the neighbors' houses were already lit for Christmas. Tom hadn't walked the street to gauge the competition, but from what he could see of the surrounding ten or so houses, all but Richard's were decorated. The one across the way had life-size gingerbread men standing on the lawn, with multi-colored lights running along every door, window, and corner of the house. Tom thought the resemblance to a gingerbread house was clever, but certainly not something that would blow anyone's socks off.

The one next to that had a lit wreath on every window and door. Eighteen total. Simple, yet elegant, but also too basic to be considered competition.

The one on the other side had dozens of Christmas trees lit with white lights along the front lawn, and white lights along the windows and roof. Nothing to worry about.

A house further down had giant snowflakes on a wire that literally stretched above the street to the house directly across from it. People would have to drive under the giant snowflakes if they wanted to go down the street. Nice effort, but not nice enough.

Several of the other houses had a mix of white and green and red lights, mostly around trees, bushes, and windows.

All in all, some very nice displays, but none were as good as what Tom was about to do.

He made one final round through the yard, checking extension cords and timers. He wanted it to go off without a hitch. Evan and Brittany waited anxiously in the front yard while Trevor struggled to pull Noel away from the kitchen.

"Okay, let's see what you've done," Noel said as she made her way to the kids.

The sun set over the rolling foothills, giving way to a cool night. Evan and Brittany bundled up in their jackets. Trevor and Noel wore sweaters. Tom hadn't gone inside the house in more than three hours, and although it was getting cold, he wasn't going to stop now.

"Ready, Grandpa?" Trevor asked.

Tom checked the timer on the final outlet, then he stood up, feeling the stiffness throughout his entire body. He glanced down at his watch, thirty seconds left. He hurried to the sidewalk where Noel and the kids stood, and he turned to watch the house. Suddenly, one vertical line of green lights lit up along the very far right of the house. The rest of the house and yard stayed dark. Trevor turned and asked what was wrong, but Tom ignored him.

The next second the line went dark and the next line of lights beside it lit up. Then in rapid succession, the lights flashed on, one row at a time. A wave of red and green zoomed across the front of the house and continued along the side. The kids ran to watch the wave of lights skip over to the detached garage. Next thing they knew, the lights on the roof flashed on and began a wave back along the side of the house. Tom could hear their oohs and aahs as the lights ran along the side of the house, following the wave. Soon the wave hit the roof along the front of the house and continued across. When the last red strand blinked off, the next one to go on was the bushes bordering Richard's lawn. Then the bushes flashed off and the first tall oak tree flashed on in a brilliant red-and-green mix. The next tree blinked on. Then the next. The bushes at the other end had their turn, illuminating red before finally, all the lights came on.

"Wow," Trevor said quietly, staring in awe at what they'd just seen.

"That was incredible," Noel said.

"Not done yet," Tom replied.

Tom hurried across the lawn to the side of the house. Noel and the kids followed. His legs ached after being on his feet all day, but now wasn't the time to give up. He pushed through the pain until he reached the garage on the side of the house. The garage door was the only part of the house facing the street that wasn't covered in lights; Tom had something else in store for it.

Suddenly, the projector he'd set up next to the sidewalk clicked into motion. Tom watched as Noel studied it, moving curiously toward the machine as it roared to life. A second later, a stream of light projected out onto the wall. He looked back over to Noel, whose eyes darted toward the garage.

Displayed against the old, white, wooden garage door on the side of the house was a black and white movie. The film started with a shot of a downtown at night, with snow falling.

An elderly voice played over the projector: "I owe everything to George Bailey."

The film panned to a house with more snow falling, then another, then another. With each house, a new voice asked God to help George Bailey. Tom saw the surprise recognition in Noel's expression. It was the start to her mother's favorite movie, *It's a Wonderful Life*. The movie shot to an image of stars. The kids' eyes glued to the garage door as well. Tom glanced back over at Noel and saw her tears welling up in her eyes, glistening from the lights. She stared, entranced, and Tom couldn't look away from her. A moment later, Noel looked in his direction expectantly. Tom felt his face go hot and he looked down, but he could feel Noel continue to watch him. It was a long moment before she finally turned her attention back to the movie. Tom knew that Noel was reading into his choice of movie, but there was no need for that. Even if it was Holly's favorite, *It's a Wonderful Life* was simply a good movie, and he just wanted to win.

Tom let out a long breath and stood back by the tree in silence as the kids watched the movie. The lights went off, and a moment later the wave began again. He had them on a loop to repeat the cycle every three minutes. He had to admit, the light show had turned out even better than he'd expected. He'd seen a few pesky bulbs that hadn't lit up, but he'd fix those in the daylight tomorrow.

A car came driving down the street, and as it approached Tom's house and the movie playing on the garage door, it slowed to a stop.

Tom couldn't quite see who was inside, but he could at least see that they'd stopped to see what was playing. Judging by the quick stop, combined with Noel's and the kids' reactions, he guessed that the movie would be a hit. Who didn't love *It's a Wonderful Life*? It was a classic, and Tom had a feeling several more cars would be making their way over to his home on the corner of Hidden Meadows Lane to check out his display.

Now he just had to hope no one would one-up him before the December 22nd winner's announcement ceremony.

CHAPTER 11

FRIDAY, DECEMBER 11

I saw your display last night."

Tom looked up from the shorted bulb he'd been working on to face the old raspy voice. He rose slowly out of his crouch when he saw Richard hobbling up the lawn without Christie in hand.

"You aren't playing around this year."

"No, I'm not," Tom said. "Finally gonna win that stupid Cup, and show that Garcetti family money doesn't buy you everything."

"You might actually have a shot. Unless I have something to say about it." Richard stood back, watching Tom work his magic on the strand. "This might surprise you, but I'm not here for you."

"Oh, yeah?" Tom asked.

"Yeah, I want to talk to that tall grandson of yours."

"*Trevor*? What for?"

"I'm not feeling a hundred percent today. Dang chest feels heavy. And like I told you, I'm entering the competition. I could pay him for the hand."

Tom and Richard didn't talk health when they could avoid it, so hearing Richard mention not feeling a hundred percent told Tom something was up.

"Trevor!" Tom yelled.

"Yeah, Grandpa?" the boy called from the distance.

Tom's foot had gone numb, but he tried not to make it obvious as he backed up to look up to the roof. Richard glanced up as well. Above, the gray clouds swirled quickly, looking as though the impending rainstorm was about to start.

"Hi, Trevor," Richard rasped.

Trevor nodded down at him from the top of the roof. He was wearing black pants again with the same porcupine-spiked hair, but this time he was also wearing a red and green striped sweater. Tom didn't know what it meant, but he certainly wasn't going to complain. A little color in the boy's life would do him some good. Trevor clutched the chimney for support while setting down a bulb he'd been working on.

Tom had shown him how to repair and replace bulbs earlier, and surprisingly, Trevor had been a quick learner. Tom remembered struggling for hours back in his early days training to be an electrician. Maybe Trevor would become one someday too. A kid that sharp could probably do whatever he wanted when the time came.

"Your grandpa told me you might be able to lend me a hand? I'm hoping to put up some lights of my own, and well, see, my back isn't what it used to be. Frankly, neither is the rest of me. Anyway, was hoping you might be able to help me give your grandpa a little competition. I can pay you, of course."

Trevor looked to Tom, trying to gauge his reaction.

"Don't worry. Richard won't beat us," Tom assured him with a smile.

"Don't be so sure," Richard rebutted.

They looked up to Trevor.

"So, what do you say?" Tom asked.

"Okay." Trevor nodded, and without a second's hesitation, he backed down the roof until he reached the ladder.

Tom limped over and grabbed the ladder before Trevor began to climb down.

Trevor followed Richard as he hobbled across the grass.

Tom couldn't help but think about the old days and how asking for help from the competition would have been unheard of. It didn't matter if you had a limb hanging from your body—you just didn't do it. Tom would work on his house as long as it took without any help, and Richard on his. Back then, Tom could climb a ladder or a tree like it was nothing. Back then, Richard could run from one side of his yard to the other in a few seconds. Today, everything was different. Both men, once limber, resilient and fast, were now slow, unbalanced, and getting weaker by the day. It wasn't something Tom liked to admit, but seeing Richard ask for help was just another subtle reminder that things were not as they once were.

A few hours later, Tom walked over for a look at their work. The sun was setting in the background, leaving a gray-and-purple haze in the sky. Soon, the houses on the street would be flipping on their Christmas lights.

Richard didn't have a corner house like Tom, which meant he didn't have to decorate both the front and the side of the house. Less square footage was both a blessing and a curse; it was less work to cover the house and lower electricity costs. But it also meant less space to make a spectacular display and less of a chance of winning the Cup. It wasn't a secret that the houses that had won in the past were, for the most part, what one would call large.

Icicle lights lined Richard's eaves. The windows and doors of his one-story home had strings of small white lights around them. It appeared as though Trevor had also helped string white lights along the rosebushes and the tall oak tree out front. The icing on Richard's cake was the white snowflake lights hanging from the branches of the tree. Tom guessed that Trevor must have climbed the tree in order to hang them so high up.

A white winter wonderland theme. All together not a bad effort.

"Ah, good. You came to meet your doom," Richard said, hobbling out of his front door, then down the steps.

"I don't know, Richard, maybe you were right. This might be your year after all," Tom said playfully.

Trevor took a seat on the grass of the front lawn.

Richard's grass was quite a bit greener than Tom's, although Tom didn't see why Richard even cared. His wife was gone too, and the only person who was going to see it regularly was Richard himself.

Tom noticed some bottles in Richard's hands as he made his way up the front lawn.

"Care to join us for a Coke?" Richard wheezed.

"Sure." Tom grabbed a glass-bottled Coke from Richard, then struggled to take a seat on the grass beside Trevor. He knew that glass-bottled Coke had been Marlene's favorite. On several birthdays and

Christmases, Holly had given them to her as gifts. The bottles weren't cheap, and Marlene collected them religiously, along with all sorts of other Coke memorabilia. Glass-bottled Coke had become a special occasion thing for Marlene and Richard, which made Tom wonder if Richard considered this a some sort of special occasion.

"Thank you, Richard," Trevor said politely as Richard handed him a glass bottle too.

Richard shook slightly while bending over to have a seat on the grass beside them.

They each popped off the top and then chugged their sodas.

Tom glanced across the street toward the purple and gray sunset. A California winter chill hung in the air, but something in the moment felt right. The crisp, sweet cola went down smooth as Tom took another sip. The carbonation bubbled against his tongue, making him feel warm inside. He let out a long breath, then glanced over to Richard who also sat staring up at the sunset while nursing his Coke. Richard's wispy white hair looked even fainter in the light, and his aged, wrinkled skin appeared even older.

Trevor smiled a casual smile while taking a big chug of his Coke. His bottle was nearly empty, and it was obvious that Trevor saw the Coke as something to quench his thirst, as opposed to something to savor and enjoy. "This reminds me of a few years back helping my dad put up lights," the boy said, interrupting the silence.

Tom and Richard glanced at each other, both wondering if the other was going to be the one to reply to his statement. When Richard gave Tom a slight shoulder shrug, Tom realized he'd have to be the one to take it on. He cleared his throat.

"Oh, yeah?" was all Tom could think to say.

"Yeah," Trevor answered. "We used to decorate too. Not as nice as this though." He gestured to Richard's house behind them.

"I liked your dad," Richard said.

Trevor looked up, surprised. "You knew my dad?"

Richard laughed. "Of course. He and Noel used to come by all the time. In fact, Jacob lived right up the street when he first moved to town. Did you know that?"

Trevor shook his head.

"I was at the house helping Tom with something, probably teaching him how to be a man like I usually was, when Jacob came over to meet with Noel for the first time after school. He said it was to study, but Tom and I had our doubts, didn't we?"

Tom let out a soft laugh, remembering that day like it was yesterday. He had been about to tell Jacob to take a hike before he'd seen the look in Noel's eyes. She hadn't been a particularly popular girl, and Tom couldn't remember any boys having ever come over. As much as Tom wanted to shut the door on Jacob, he knew he couldn't do that to Noel.

"He was a good kid," Tom said. "Good man, too."

Trevor stayed silent.

When Tom and Holly received the news about Jacob's cancer, they'd offered to do anything they could to help. Jacob and Noel never asked for money, but on several occasions they did ask for babysitting. Evan had been a newborn back then, and Holly didn't hesitate even for a second in rushing over to help. When they'd lost Jacob, a big part of the family had been torn away. He'd become one of them, as much as Tom might have tried to deny it at the time. Tom had always liked Jacob, but he'd never gone out of his way to show it.

But as hard as it had been to lose Jacob, it was even harder to deal with their loss of Noel. Not physically, of course, but she had died emotionally. She'd uprooted the kids and shut herself off. She declined offers to move home every time Tom and Holly had asked. She had life insurance money, but Tom knew she had to be struggling. She'd check in with him and Holly from time to time, but she really wanted to try to find a new place where she and the kids could start new. Then there was Bryan, the guy who looked an awful lot like Jacob, even sounded like him too. When Bryan had gotten that job in Sacramento, Noel and the kids had moved even further away.

Tom contemplated continuing the conversation, but when he turned back to Trevor and Richard, he noticed that they were both lost in the clouds while holding their bottles of Coke. Tom joined them once more, and together they watched as the setting sun gave way to the cool winter night.

Sometimes the best conversations were the ones that went unsaid.

That evening, Tom stared out past the windowsill as another car slowed to watch the lights. It had only been dark out for an hour, and already over a hundred cars had stopped to look. Many of them had parked on the side of the house to watch *It's a Wonderful Life*. He knew the idea would reel them in. People had driven by to check out his displays in the past, but never like this.

"There's another one!" Brittany called from the entryway.

Each of the kids were hiding behind windows, watching the onlookers as they drove by. None of them could believe the amount of attention the house was already getting.

Clearly, word got around fast in Glenn Hills.

Noel couldn't help but laugh as she was doing dishes while watching the kids and Tom continuing to gaze out the windows.

CHAPTER 12

SATURDAY, DECEMBER 12

Nothing puts you in the Christmas spirit quicker than rain, Christmas music, and the smell of fresh hot cocoa.

Noel topped the mug with whipped cream and slid it across the counter.

"Thanks," the woman said, slipping a dollar into the tip jar and then making her way over to a table in the corner.

A jazzy rendition of "Rockin' Around the Christmas Tree" popped on as the rain continued to splash hard against the window. Noel smiled and hummed along as she wiped down the countertop.

"Someone's happy today."

Noel turned toward the sound of Tate's deep voice coming from behind her.

"Yeah. It's starting to really feel like Christmas. Don't you love it?"

Tate walked over to the countertop and glanced out at the rain. "Not when it scares away customers."

"Okay, I'll give you that. You heading out soon? I thought Josephine normally worked Saturdays since she was in school during the week?"

"Nope. She had to study today, so you're stuck with me." Tate pulled a red mug out from the stack. "I thought I'd get to know you better, actually. I like to get to know my employees. So tell me, who is Noel VanHansen?"

Noel put her hands on her hips in mock skepticism. "The almighty Tate wants to get to know the common folk, does he?"

Tate filled his mug with black coffee. "The almighty Tate, huh? I'm not that bad, am I?"

Noel laughed. "No, I'm just playing. You've actually been great. So what do you want to know?"

Tate rubbed his beard as though pondering it. "Hmm, let's see. Well, for starters, what brought you to Glenn Hills?"

Noel took a deep breath. Not exactly the conversation she wanted to have with her boss. "You had to start with the hardest question?"

"Sorry, you don't have to answer if it's too difficult."

Noel lifted her hand to cut him off. "No, it's okay. The truth is that I had a messy divorce and we had nowhere to go. So we moved in with my father."

Tate's smile dropped to a look of embarrassment. "Oh, wow. Dumb boss move. I'm sorry, I didn't mean to bring that up."

"It's fine. We're here, and we're making the best of it."

Tate nodded. "At least you have your father for support. I'm sure that helps."

Noel let out a reluctant laugh. "I wish. My father is about as emotionally supportive as a rock. I mean, I guess he's coming around a little bit, but he can't wait for us to move out."

As she said it, she thought about the beautiful display her father had put together. He could say he did it to win the Christmas Cup. He could even say he did it for the kids. But Noel knew exactly why he'd done it, even if he wouldn't ever admit it. He'd done it for Holly. Noel still didn't know what really happened that night she died, and it seemed as though Tom might never tell her. But one thing was clear: he still loved Holly dearly. To Noel, it was a sign that he cared more than he let on, and that maybe he was actually changing.

"Wow, I'm really striking out, aren't I?" Tate shook his head. Noel looked back up and smiled, pulled away from her thoughts. He continued. "You know what, maybe I shouldn't be the one asking the questions."

"Really, it's fine." Noel liked the way he tried to lighten the mood. Even if these weren't easy things to talk about, talking with him felt natural. "My mother died two years ago, and my father and I had a bit of a falling out over it. Since then, he's become a different man altogether. He's always rude and he's always trying to sneak into another room.

But, surprisingly, he agreed to help the kids decorate for the Christmas Cup Competition."

"Oh, really?" Tate asked. "You know I'm supposed to be a judge for it this year?"

"Yup. My father told me. Wanted me to try to coerce you into voting for him."

They laughed.

"Well," Tate said, "you can tell him that as a judge, I will at least take his house into consideration. From what I've heard, they hire a big bus for the judges to see literally every house in the city. Takes a couple of nights to see them all."

Noel brushed loose coffee beans on the counter into her palm. "I'll let him know. Are you and your wife going to enter? Or are judges not allowed?"

Tate hesitated a moment. Then he took a deep breath.

Noel immediately realized she'd crossed a boundary. Asking about significant others had to be some sort of rule you weren't supposed to break in the workplace. It had just slipped out. "Sorry. Now I'm the one who messed up. I shouldn't have asked that."

"No, no. It's fine." Tate held up his left hand to touch his ring. His eyes stayed glued to it as he continued. "Alice passed away a year and a half ago. It's just me. And no, I'm not able to win since I'm a judge. I'd guess that would be considered a conflict of interest."

"Oh, Tate, I'm so sorry." She contemplated putting her hand on his shoulder for support, but decided against it.

Tate looked up and laughed. "We're both really good at making conversation, aren't we?"

"Guess so," she said, laughing herself. "If you ever need someone to talk to about it, I'm here. I know what it's like to lose loved ones."

Tate's eyes met hers, and they lingered for a long moment.

In that moment, Noel felt a connection with the man. The truth was that as supportive as people were about her losing Jacob, only those who had lost their spouses too would ever truly know how it felt. And something about the moment left Noel with a profound sense of comfort. Like Tate truly understood her. Like he was gazing through her eyes and into her heart. She also felt slightly less guilty with herself for noticing his good looks now that she knew he wasn't a married man anymore. Finally, he looked up as the door sprang open, and a slender woman around Noel's age in a yellow rain jacket walked in.

Outside, the rain continued to beat down against the ground and window. Water spewed across the floor as the woman closed her umbrella.

"Sorry!" she said.

Tate put on that famous lumberjack smile customers fell for every time. "No problem. There's an umbrella holder next to the door. What can we get started for you?"

The woman set the umbrella in the holder and glanced toward Tate, smiling back a shy smile. Noel knew that smile; the woman was flirting. It's all in the eyes, and this woman knew how to work it. Noel wasn't really surprised. Tate was an attractive man, and when he put on the charm, it was nearly impossible not to notice.

"What do *you* recommend?" she asked, her voice sultrier than it needed to be.

Tate glanced over to Noel. "Noel makes a mean gingerbread hot cocoa."

The woman didn't even glance at Noel for the slightest of seconds. "If that's what you recommend," she crooned.

Tate chuckled. "You won't be disappointed." He leaned in to whisper to Noel as the woman reached into her purse. "Pressure's on. Better be good."

Noel laughed.

When the woman handed Tate her card, however, Noel noticed that her hand lingered on Tate's for an extra second, her eyes never leaving his.

Noel shrugged to herself, then reached for a mug to make the gingerbread cocoa. She wasn't sure whether Tate had meant the pressure was on because he wanted to impress the woman in the cute and expensive looking yellow raincoat, or simply because she was a customer. She unwittingly felt a pang of jealousy toward the woman who'd obviously gotten Tate's attention. But then she reminded herself again of what'd happened the last time she'd let men back into her life.

Tate was her boss, not another man for her to cling onto. Plus, he'd literally just told her about his wife. Did she have no shame at all?

Noel pushed it from her mind, put on a smile, and reminded herself she was lucky to even have a job. She pulled out the gingerbread crumbs to get to work on the cup of hot cocoa.

Tom had never seen this many cars outside his house in all the years he'd lived there. Not one of his Christmas displays from the past years had beckoned even half this many cars. And in the rain!

He watched through the window as more and more cars pulled up along the side of his house. People sat and watched *It's a Wonderful Life* from their cars. Others even walked the sidewalk under their umbrellas, watching the wave of red and green Christmas lights race across the house.

Trevor, Brittany, and Evan watched the crowd from the living room window a few feet over.

Noel laughed as she walked in from the kitchen. "You know you should be watching the lights, not the people, right?" she whispered.

"Shhhh, Mom, they might hear you," Brittany whispered back.

Noel laughed again, shook her head, and then walked into the other room.

Just like the kids, Tom couldn't look away. The people just kept on coming! Everyone watched with awe: kids, toddlers, teens, adults, even seniors, all fully equipped in their winter wear.

For the first time in his life, Tom actually believed they might win this thing.

If only Holly could see it now.

CHAPTER 13

SUNDAY, DECEMBER 13

Tom and Trevor had spent the entire day in the yard fixing bulbs that had mysteriously gone out the night before. The sporadic California rain had disappeared again, leaving them with a brief window to fix the display before the next round of onlookers came to see their house that evening.

Brittany and Evan waved from across the brick wall by Richard's house.

"We're back, Grandpa!" Evan shouted while he, Brittany, Christie, and Richard strolled up the lawn.

"You see that crowd outside my house last night?" Richard asked. "Looks like I'm actually gonna win this thing."

Tom laughed as he glanced up from the bulb he'd been working on. "The only reason those people were outside your house was because the parking in front of mine was full."

Richard waved him off. "That's what we call denial."

Christie barked twice, wagging her curly white tail as she approached Tom.

"Fine, I admit it. They came to see you." Tom stuck out his tongue and reached down slowly to pet Christie, and she immediately rubbed her head into his palm.

"You should see Evan and Brittany with her. These kids are naturals," Richard said as Tom rose back up, the blood in his head making him slightly dizzy.

"Humph," Tom grumbled.

Evan and Brittany grinned from ear to ear at the compliment.

"I hope we can get a dog like Christie for Christmas," Brittany said.

Tom shot a telling glance at Richard. Didn't he realize that he was getting the kids' hopes up?

Richard simply shrugged. "When do the judges come by anyway?" he asked as Tom moved on to fixing another bulb.

The sun had almost set over the foothills, leaving the sky a darkening purple, which meant the time for small talk was rapidly dwindling. Only a few more minutes until Christmas goers would be arriving. "They do their bus tour next weekend and announce the winner a few days before Christmas. Now sorry to cut this party short, but some of us have to get back to decorating."

"I'm telling you, I already have it in the bag. They tell me it's a lock. You're better off putting up a lawn chair outside my house to watch it happen."

Tom shook his head.

"Okay, Christie, let's go. We obviously aren't wanted here," Richard said. "See you tomorrow, kids."

"Bye, Richard! Bye, Christie!" Evan shouted.

"Bye, Richard!" Brittany added as Richard and Christie headed home.

Trevor climbed down from the ladder as the sun began to disappear over the horizon.

"All done, Grandpa."

Noel approached from around the corner before Tom could reply.

"Mommy's home!" Brittany called. She and Evan ran to Noel for a big hug.

"Hey, guys," Noel said cheerily, reaching down to hug them both. She glanced up at Tom. "Hey, Tom, Tate gave me some extra cocoa and cups from the coffee shop. If you wanted, I thought I could whip up some cocoa with Mom's old recipe to hand out to the people that come by. Could help your chances of winning."

"Hmm" was all Tom said. It wasn't a bad idea, but couldn't anyone tell he was busy?

He continued his last-minute preparations with Trevor at his side until the sun vanished, giving way to a crisp, cool winter night. After one last bulb, Tom and Trevor stood back. Several of the houses along their street had flipped their Christmas lights on, transforming Hidden Meadows Lane into a vibrant Christmas spectacle. Cars began to roll up to the house, parking out front. Tom counted eight by the time he glanced down at his watch to see how much longer until the timers flipped on their own light show. Two more minutes.

"Evening!" called a man from behind them.

Tom turned to see who was talking to him. And then he saw them getting out of an SUV. The regal family from the newspaper, the Garcettis. Alex, Tom remembered from the garage sale, with his wife and two daughters. Tom gave him a quick insincere wave.

Trevor's eyes went wide at the sight.

Several more cars pulled up alongside the house, and several more people got out, ready for the light show to begin.

"Hi, Trevor," the older girl said. Her curly black hair was pulled into a ponytail, and she wore a red peacoat with a white scarf and gloves to match. In fact, all of them were wearing matching winter wear, just like they had in the picture in the newspaper.

Trevor gulped nervously. "Oh, hi, Kayla."

Alex and his wife looked over the dead grass Tom called his front lawn. Tom even thought he saw Alex's wife staring at the termite-infested black hole in the middle of the eave.

Should mind her own business.

Tom could immediately tell that Trevor was embarrassed. His cheeks flushed bright red as he took a step back, and then he turned to face the house, pretending to work on a light. Several more families parked alongside the house, waiting for the spectacle to begin. Tom glanced back at his watch, realizing it was time.

Seconds later, the single strand lit at the far right side of the house. Audible oohs and aahs sounded from the sidewalk. The first strand went dark, and instantaneously, the second one lit up. Then the wave began in rapid succession as red and green lights went on and off one by one. Soon, the wave turned the corner, and children ran along the side of the house as it continued to the other side. Then the lights reached the roof and started back down to the front of the house again.

People cheered and clapped as the wave shot along the roof. When it finally reached the end, the entire house lit up at the same time. The next moment, the movie projector popped on for another showing of *It's a Wonderful Life*.

"Wow!" a kid screamed from the side of the house.

Several of the families made their way over as more cars parked on the street. There had to be nearly a hundred people already.

"That's a heck of a show you got there," Alex said from behind Tom. Tom turned to see Alex and Kayla standing behind him, both smiling wide. "I thought I told you that you could only buy our lights if you weren't going to beat us this year." Alex laughed when Tom glared back at him. "I'm kidding. But really, you did a great job."

Tom nodded. Tom didn't feel Alex was being genuine. He didn't like the man. Alex walked over to the side of the house to catch up to his wife.

"This is amazing," Kayla said.

Tom looked over to see her approaching Trevor across the grass.

"Really?" Trevor said nervously.

"Yeah. It's so pretty." She reached over and touched Trevor's arm when he looked down nervously. "I hope you win."

Trevor looked up with a shy smile, unable to meet her eyes.

A second later, Kayla's hand dropped, and she walked off with a smile to meet her family at the side of the house.

Tom couldn't help but wonder if she'd meant it. The Garcettis' own daughter thought they should win?

Trevor twiddled his fingers as he watched her go. *Could he be any more obvious?*

"Do you think we'll win, Grandpa? I don't know what we're going to do if we don't win that money. My mom really needs help, and I thought if we won, maybe we could give her the help she needs."

Tom looked down at the boy, finally understanding his motivations. It wasn't just to celebrate Christmas. Trevor was worried about his mother and finances, and this was his way of looking after his family. Tom inhaled a long and deep breath. "We'll see," he finally said.

Together, they walked around the side of the house to see the crowd watching the movie.

Noel approached with a tray of hot cocoas moments later. Evan and Brittany grabbed them and helped her pass them out to the onlookers.

Not a bad touch, Tom thought, watching the smiles grow across everyone's faces as they sipped on rich hot cocoa while watching *It's a Wonderful Life*, with the light show going on in the background. He was pretty certain that if Holly were around, she would have done the same thing. Noel reminded Tom of Holly more and more each time he saw her. He supposed it was part of the reason he'd been fine with pushing Noel out of his life, all the subtle reminders of the woman he'd loved. He tried to force the thought from his mind as he made his way through the crowd. The frigid night air was growing colder by the minute, and his sweet tooth craved the taste of a sweet, rich hot cocoa.

Noel was standing next to a group of four women, all dressed to the nines as though they were going to the ballet or some sort of black tie affair. Tom realized one of the women was that Alex Garcetti's wife. He made his way closer, inconspicuously trying to listen to their conversation.

"It's so cute what you guys are trying to do here," the Garcetti woman said.

Noel narrowed her eyes. "Thanks for coming by," she returned before turning to hand out more hot cocoas.

Tom was about to approach them when suddenly the woman lifted a hand into the air.

"Excuse me," she shouted for everyone around them to hear. The onlookers turned to face her, forming a circle around the group of women. She put on a smile, which looked absolutely fake.

Noel glanced back at Tom for a second, and Tom thought he saw her shoulders drop slightly before she turned to face the woman.

"As many of you know, I'm Samantha Garcetti, winner of the last five Glenn Hills Christmas Cup Competitions." The three women next to her burst into applause, and the rest of the crowd did as well. Samantha gave another fake laugh and waved them off. "Oh, stop it," she said playfully. "Any who, we just wanted to announce that the lighting ceremony for our brand new Christmas display will start tomorrow at 6 p.m. Trust me when I say you won't want to miss it."

More cheers and applause erupted from the crowd.

Samantha smiled wide and waved as she ate it all up.

Noel handed the tray to Trevor and made her way through the crowd, up the driveway, and then out of sight. Evan and Brittany followed behind her.

Tom watched as Samantha found Alex, who gave her a dubious look. Kayla approached, shrugging, embarrassment in her expression.

Tom had seen enough, and he was about to tell her to leave when someone tugged at his elbow.

A woman, probably in her forties with graying black hair and a cozy-looking wool jacket, smiled up at him and then leaned in. "I hope you guys beat her," she said.

Tom nodded, grumbling. "Thanks."

The woman turned back to watch the movie, and when Tom looked over to find Samantha, she was gone. Alex led the way, walking back down the sidewalk with Samantha, Kayla, and their second daughter in tow. Samantha's pack of friends also made their way to their cars. It seemed their mission was done.

Tom had never wanted to win the Christmas Cup Competition more than he did in that moment.

It was just nine days until the winner's announcement ceremony.

CHAPTER 14

MONDAY, DECEMBER 14

W e're going to miss it!" Trevor shouted anxiously from the back
seat of the Bronco.

Tom ignored him and Noel as she looked toward the eighteen-mile-
an-hour readout on the speedometer. He stayed silent and focused on
the road ahead. A few minutes later, they approached the street.

"Holy Moses," Tom said under his breath.

On the street in front of them, there had to be over two hundred
cars parked along the sides. Flocks of people walked the sidewalk toward
the Garcettis' massive white mansion.

"We're going to miss it!" Trevor shouted again.

"We'll make it, honey." Tom saw Noel glance down at the clock.
5:51 p.m. Nine minutes until the lighting began.

Tom reversed out of the street and found a spot within a couple of
blocks. Around them, several more cars pulled into slots while people
jogged down the sidewalk. The crowd outside Tom's house the night
before may have been big, but it was nothing compared to this. Even the
garage sale the Garcettis had put on the week before hadn't come close
to the enormity of the crowd today.

"Everyone got their coats and gloves?" Noel asked as Tom turned
off the headlights and then the engine. She pulled a pair of white gloves
from her purse, and put on a white beanie to match. In the rearview
mirror, Tom saw each of the kids holding up their gloves as well. "What
about you, Tom?"

Tom scoffed. "I don't need gloves. I'm an adult." He opened the door and leapt out.

"It's going to be cold," she warned.

The kids hopped out directly after him.

Trevor led the pack, practically darting down the sidewalk.

Tom followed behind Trevor, Noel, and the kids as another family tried to hurry past them.

"Come on, guys!" Trevor said while turning back to see Tom at least a hundred feet behind him.

Tom rolled his eyes and kept his pace. A shiver ran up his spine as a blast of cold wind whipped across his exposed neck.

Noel glanced back right as Tom was about to pull his sleeves over his hands.

Tom released the sleeves and continued on as though nothing was wrong.

They saw at least two hundred people bundled up in their winter wear when they turned the corner, impatiently waiting for the moment the show would begin. Trevor waved them in as he hurried toward the crowd. Tom huddled next to Noel and the kids as each faced forward to watch the show begin.

The house stayed dark another minute more as children around them jittered with excitement for the Christmas spectacle they were about to behold.

Finally, it began. An array of white lights burst into action, casting a spotlight upon the white marble mansion. A trumpet began to play, loud for all to hear. All eyes shot to the top of the roof, where a giant snowman had been illuminated from a spotlight below. Next, a bell began to chime, and the spotlight shifted to the center of the roof where a bronze bell moved back and forth.

Within seconds, the lyrics began:

"Sleigh bells ring, are you listening? In the lane, snow is glistening. A beautiful sight, we're happy tonight, walking in a winter wonderland."

The entire house exploded with white lights all at once, nearly every inch of the exterior covered. A loud boom rang in the air. Suddenly, the sky was covered in white.

Tom knew what they were the second he glanced up at them: snowflakes.

The crowd erupted into a deafening cheer.

Tom glanced from side to side to see everyone staring up with their jaws dropped in utter astonishment. He had to give it to them; he was astonished too.

The crowd began to move after the display. Trevor, Noel, Brittany, and Evan followed suit. It took a second before Tom caught up with them. As the crowd moved, the spotlight shot from one window of the mansion where a shadow of Santa Claus waved, to another where a reindeer's nose glowed red, then another where elves jumped up and down. Soon, they were funneling through a massive cast-iron gate that led into the backyard.

Christmas trees all decorated in white lights lined the way. The scene grew loud around him as everyone began to whisper to one another about all the beautiful decorations around the property, and the music continued to hum. Then audible gasps and children's cheers erupted from ahead.

Trevor and the kids ran toward whatever the crowd had gathered around. People behind Tom tried to nudge him forward as he struggled to get there.

"Hold your horses," Tom croaked to the crowd around him.

The song ended, and what sounded like someone tapping on a microphone took hold. More spotlights shone ahead to a platform where another snow machine was pumping out flakes. Tom noticed a person on top of the platform. He squinted as the spotlight fixed on him, and suddenly everyone cheered. A man with rosy red cheeks, a white beard, red cap, and red coat stood, waving to the crowd.

"Ho, Ho, Ho!" he bellowed in a deep, jolly voice.

"Santa!" kids screamed.

Trevor, Brittany, and Evan stepped forward, and finally Tom saw that they were all looking at a magnificent large ice rink. Tom guessed the rink had to be nearly a hundred feet wide on either side. Several kids and their parents hurried to don ice skates from a booth at the front of the line. Tom tried to compute all of the wiring they'd had to do for such a spectacle. If he thought his house had been difficult, the Garcettis' had to be near impossible.

"Hello, everyone!" someone said loud into the microphone.

Tom glanced up, recognizing the voice. Standing next to Santa on the platform above the snow machine was Alex Garcetti, wearing a red knit sweater and a white scarf, with his hair perfectly groomed to the side. He smiled wide for the enormous crowd. "I just wanted to take a second to thank you all on behalf of our whole family for showing up tonight. We hope you enjoy the light show and the ice skating. Also, Santa is coming down to listen to your Christmas wishes, and we'll have Santa's little helpers coming around with free hot cocoa and rich apple cider. So have fun, and have a Merry Christmas!"

"Oh, please," Tom said, rolling his eyes. And then he saw Trevor.

The boy was looking down with a look of pure defeat. A tear dropped from his eye, which he quickly wiped away.

Noel didn't notice Trevor as she tried to calm Brittany and Evan, both clearly distracted by the growing line for the ice skating rink.

Tom approached Trevor. "Some display, huh?"

Trevor sniffled as he looked up. "Yup."

"Don't worry, ours has more heart. The judges will see through this."

As Tom said the words, he knew they weren't genuine. The Garcettis had outdone themselves and the entire town of Glenn Hills, yet again. An extravagant mansion covered in brilliant white lights. A snowman on the roof. Santa, elves, and reindeer in the windows. Christmas music on loudspeakers. Hundreds of Christmas trees, Santa, hot cocoa, apple cider, and an ice rink. And on top of it all, snow! This was something people would pay to see. Tom couldn't replicate it in a million years. Couldn't have even dreamt up such a thing. No, Tom knew that their chances of winning had greatly diminished. Who knew, maybe there would be some sympathetic judges, but the Garcettis had put on the Christmas show of a lifetime, and he was pretty certain they'd win for it, again.

"Can we go home?" Trevor asked.

Tom looked over at Noel, who was waving them over from the line down the way. Evan and Brittany jumped up and down as they watched the ice rink through the glass.

"We better wait here until they finish," Tom finally replied.

Trevor nodded slowly and followed Tom to the glass to watch and wait.

Soon enough, Noel, Evan, and Brittany joined the dozens of others on the rink. Noel waved before grabbing both Brittany's and Evan's hands, then they glided across together.

Around them, the crowd pulsed with energy, everyone taking in the snow, the lights on the house, the Christmas trees, and the ice rink. Another massive line formed around Santa's throne for the kids to make their Christmas wishes.

Tom and Trevor simply stood silent, waiting for it all to end.

"Trevor?" asked a young voice from behind them.

Tom and Trevor turned to see a girl holding out a tray of hot cocoas.

Trevor lit up. "Kayla. I mean, uh, oh, yeah. Hi." His words were a jumbled mess, but Kayla smiled a friendly smile in return.

"Would you like a hot cocoa?" she asked.

Tom smelled sweet, rich chocolate as the steam rose to meet his nose. "Sure," he grumbled.

Kayla looked up, realizing Trevor wasn't alone. She smiled and handed a cup to Tom. Tom knew he didn't need the sugar, but who could resist hot cocoa? It was cold out, after all. "Would you like one, Trevor?"

Trevor blushed. "Uh, okay. Yeah. Thanks."

Kayla handed him one as well, and their eyes lingered on each other. "Well, I better keep getting these passed out. Thanks for coming by." Tom had to admit that the girl was far nicer than he'd expected her to be, given her mother's antics. Almost seemed like someone else's daughter altogether.

Trevor nodded nervously, and Kayla turned to face the bustling crowd around them. But then she stopped and looked back for a quick second. "Oh, yeah, and I still hope you win," she said. Her eyes stayed on Trevor's for the slightest of seconds before she turned once more to meet the crowd.

Tom wondered if she was being sincere, or if it was part of some sort of competitive play. Tom wasn't sure, but one thing was clear: Trevor and Kayla both had crushes on each other. He'd seen those looks before. He'd given them to Holly some time ago. Trevor was in deep.

Trevor and Tom lifted their hot cups of cocoa to their lips and drank in unison, the warm, creamy cocoa tingling Tom's taste buds and throat as it went down smooth. They both turned back to watch Noel and the kids glide across the rink, Tom suddenly feeling a bit more optimistic than he had earlier.

CHAPTER 15

TUESDAY, DECEMBER 15

Bertha slapped a batch of mouthwatering golden-brown waffles down on the table for each of them. Tom took in the sweet smells of warm cinnamon and buttermilk.

"Eat up, boys. And fair warning, if I sense any trouble, I'm not afraid to take those waffles away." Bertha adjusted her red Christmas apron, glared at Richard, and walked off. She looked even more like Mrs. Claus than usual, her white hair pinned up with curly bangs in the front, her cheeks rosier than normal, and her red ensemble to accompany.

"I've said it a hundred times, Bertha, you won't kick us out. You'd miss our beautiful faces too much," Richard wheezed.

She scoffed loud for the entire restaurant to hear, then she strutted off into the kitchen.

Tom rolled his eyes at Richard's remark. "What would Marlene think if she saw you flirting like this?"

"What are you talking about? You did this last week too. What's gotten into you?" Richard asked. "It's nothing more than witty banter between intellectuals, something you wouldn't know much about." Richard glanced back to the kitchen.

Tom lunged for the syrup before Richard could get to it.

"Whoa there, Turbo," Richard wheezed.

"Yeah, yeah," Tom grumbled.

"What's with you asking me what Marlene would think? Bertha and I have talked like this for years. It's harmless. The better question is what would Holly think if she saw *you* like *this*?" Richard gestured toward the syrup as Tom nearly emptied the bottle over his batch of waffles.

"She'd love it," Tom said. "It means I'll see her sooner."

Tom waited for Richard to make some sort of sarcastic quip, but it didn't come.

Instead, when Tom glanced up, he saw Richard staring back. "It's not funny, Tom. You know that's what happened to Marlene. You have your family back, the family you thought you'd never see again. What would they do if you just up and died now? And did you tell Noel about it yet?"

Tom rolled his eyes once more and let out a deep breath. "Drop it, Richard. Let's just eat."

Tom cut into his waffle. He already knew he shouldn't have made the remark, but it'd still bothered him. Even if it was a joke, how could Richard go on flirting like that with another woman? Marlene had been the most caring, wonderful, giving woman, and for Richard to just forget about her made him look like a real jerk. Tom couldn't even begin to think about doing such a thing to Holly. That woman had been a saint, putting up with Tom for over fifty years. He'd been lucky to have her, just like Richard had been with Marlene. And the last thing they should be doing was showing their wives disrespect. Tom already had enough to live with after Holly's death, but Richard needed to mind his own business too. If Tom wanted to eat some sugar or skip a walk, that was for him to decide. Everyone dies eventually.

After taking a bite of his waffle, Tom realized Richard still hadn't moved. "Let's just drop it, Richard. Enough already." Tom shook his head.

Still Richard didn't reply or move.

Tom finally looked up from his waffles. Something felt wrong. "Richard?"

Richard's mouth drooped open to the right, and his eyes looked glassy, fixed on something in the distance.

"Richard?"

Richard's gaze didn't move. Suddenly, his lip began to quiver and his hands began to shake, then his head convulsed.

"Richard!" Tom shouted. He leapt up as Richard's entire body erupted into convulsions, and the next second Richard slumped to the side.

People leapt up around them, commotion rising everywhere.

Tom grabbed for Richard's arms as they stopped shaking, and his eyes drooped shut.

"Call 911!" someone screamed.

Tom's heart began to beat with fervor. His hands shook, his breath coming in quick gasps. What was happening? Was Richard okay? Tom wasn't sure, but it looked like a stroke, and a bad one at that. His mind raced for an idea of what to do. Were you supposed to hold him up? Lay him flat? Keep his mouth open? Tom didn't know. His eyes darted across the room as his mind sped into overdrive.

A woman stepped forward, coming to Richard's side. The restaurant was loud around them, and the woman was speaking, but Tom couldn't make out the words. He could only stare.

Richard's eyes stayed shut, and his body still. Was he dead? He couldn't be. They'd just been arguing two minutes before.

A few minutes later, more people came to Richard's side, and Tom vaguely realized that they were wearing blue uniforms. They asked Tom questions, but Tom couldn't comprehend. Was Tom having a stroke too? He raised his arm and moved his mouth, and all seemed fine. Tom realized he was in shock. Soon, they had Richard on a stretcher and out the door, then Tom was back sitting at his booth alone as the ambulance took off down the street.

"I hope he's all right," someone said, the voice tuning in from Tom's left.

Tom glanced over to see dozens of people around him, watching out the window. Bertha was sobbing in the corner, and several others looked distressed. Slowly, sound and feeling came back to him. And with it, the realization of what had happened to his friend did as well.

Tom waited in the waiting room for what had to be at least five hours. People moved in and out around him, but still no word from the doctors or nurses. The last time he'd been in this hospital had been the night of the accident, a night he'd tried to erase from his memory.

He still hadn't come to grips with the fact that his best friend of the past forty years might be gone. They'd been eating their regular Tuesday morning waffles at Bertha's only hours before. Richard had been his same overly sarcastic self, mentioning Tom's diabetes and heart disease and, of course, Holly, whom he knew wasn't someone they talked about over breakfast.

Yet Tom couldn't help but wonder if he'd been the reason Richard had had the stroke.

Tom had brought up Marlene after Richard's harmless flirting with Bertha, which had led Richard to put away his calm and jokey demeanor and change his tone to a much more serious Richard. If Tom hadn't done that, would Richard have been fine? What would he do if it was his fault? How could he live with himself, knowing he was responsible for another death of someone close to him?

In fact, as much as Tom didn't want to admit it, since Holly's passing, Richard had become the closest person in Tom's predictable, isolated life. Even with Noel and his grandkids in the house, Richard was still the only one who truly understood him. He understood what it was like to work for the man all your life and grapple with the good-for-nothing government the whole way through. What it was like watching the years in Glenn Hills go by as more people came and went, and more of the city changed and modernized. To grow old like he had, and lose the strength and sharpness he once had. Richard was the only person who understood what it was like to lose the love of your life after over forty years. The only person who understood and appreciated the fine pleasures of sugar and sweet delicious foods the same way he did. The only person who understood Tom's reason for pushing Noel and his family away and refusing to come clean about the truth of Holly's death.

Although Richard may not have agreed, Tom knew he was the only one who understood him at all. And now he might be gone.

"Mr. VanHansen?" a stone-faced, bearded man with glasses spoke from across the room. He wore a white lab coat and blue scrubs. Tom tried to read the man, but he showed no signs of emotion whatsoever.

"Yeah?"

The doctor scanned the waiting area, clearly noticing the dozen or so others waiting around. "Why don't you come with me?"

Never a good sign.

Tom hobbled after the doctor down the hallway until the doctor turned back, ensuring that they were alone. Ahead, several patient rooms sat on either side of the long hallway. Two nurses at the end helped a woman in a wheelchair. The hallway brought back the memories of his final night with Holly, Tom running down the hall to find her. Collapsing at her bedside. The doctors restraining him as he watched his lifeless wife lie unmoving.

"Mr. VanHansen," the doctor started, his voice steady, emotionless. "I'm afraid your friend, Richard, suffered an ischemia stroke. Essentially, this means he had a blood clot that blocked blood flow to part of the brain."

Tom waited for an explanation as to what this meant, his eyes wide in anticipation.

"We're going to keep him here for a few days so that we can observe him, run some tests, try to figure out why this happened, and prevent it from happening again."

Tom tilted his head. Was the doctor saying what he thought he was? "So, he's alive?"

"Yes, but he did suffer a major stroke. He isn't in the clear yet. We still need to see why this happened, and prevent it, or something worse, from happening again."

Tom swallowed the lump in his throat. The hall became blurry for a moment. He tried to compose himself as a burst of electricity shot through his body. His friend was alive. "Can I see him?"

"Yes. He just woke up," the doctor said. "But take it slow. He's still recovering."

When Tom nodded, the doctor led him down the hallway, past one room and then another. Each was filled with people of all sorts of different shapes, ages, colors, and sizes. Some looking better or worse than others. All with family or friends at their bedsides. As Tom walked, he couldn't help but wonder what would happen if he wound up in the hospital. Would anyone show up for him? For the last two years, he'd pushed away his family for just that reason.

Finally, they reached a room at the end. A heartbeat monitor chirped evenly as the doctor gestured to the doorway.

"You've got a visitor," the doctor announced, glancing in.

Tom took a deep breath, bracing himself, and then walked in.

Inside, a small window looked out to the parking lot. An IV stand and a heart monitor sat beside the raised hospital bed at the center of the room. Richard lay atop the bed in a blue gown. A wrinkled grin stretched across his face as he saw Tom—the same annoying smile he always had, which had to be a good sign.

"Look what the cat dragged in," he rasped, his voice sounding shakier and weaker than normal.

Tom glanced down at his brown flannel and worn-out old jeans and boots, trying to gather his composure. Richard's skinny, wrinkled arms protruding from a loose hospital gown wasn't something he'd expected to see in a million years. He looked weak, fragile.

"You don't look so good yourself," Tom finally said, glancing back up.

The doctor slipped out, leaving Tom and Richard alone in the room. A heavy silence hung in the air.

"Have a seat," Richard said. "You're making me nervous."

Tom glanced over to a chair between Richard's bed and another empty bed beside him. He pulled it out and took a seat in the uncomfortable plastic chair at Richard's side. "So, you're all right?"

The heartbeat monitor chirped slightly faster. "That was nothing. I'm fine. They're just keeping me here as a precaution."

Tom knew Richard was downplaying it. He'd seen the stroke himself. It certainly hadn't been nothing. "Well, I paid the bill, if that was what you were going for," Tom joked.

Richard laughed but then burst into a coughing fit. The heartbeat monitor spiked until a few seconds later, when Richard began to calm. "These fools think I need to be here for a few days. I was hoping you wouldn't mind checking on Christie. I know how you feel about animals in the house, and Christie will be fine at home, but she does need to be let out a couple times a day."

"I'll handle it," Tom said. "I'm sure the kids will be happy to help."

"Thanks." Richard turned to glance out the window into the parking lot where several cars were parked. The scene was almost like a picture with how motionless it stayed. Not even wind blowing the trees. "You need to tell Noel."

Tom looked up. "Yeah, someone will have to explain why Christie needs so much attention."

"No," Richard said. "You know what I'm talking about."

Tom didn't want to have this conversation, and at the hospital of all places? After all, they were here for Richard, not Tom.

"I'm serious, Tom. You take for granted what it means to have Noel and those kids. Marlene and I weren't ever that lucky."

"You didn't want kids," Tom countered. "What are you talking about?"

Richard's eyes narrowed and brows furrowed. "Really? You think that's true? Marlene was a teacher, for crying out loud. She surrounded herself with children because we couldn't have our own. Are you really that naive?"

Tom looked down, refusing to answer him.

"You have to tell her. She deserves to know. If you don't, I will."

Tom leapt up from his seat. "No, you won't! You promised me!"

Richard stuck his finger out at him. "I'm not going to sit by watching you waste away your life like this. Noel came back. You didn't think it would happen, but it did. There's a reason for it, and you need to tell her before it's too late and you don't get another chance."

Tom huffed loudly.

"Plus, my time's coming. I miss Marlene more and more every day. She's calling me, Tom. So if you don't think I'll do it, you're dead wrong."

Tom hated the direction the conversation had taken. In all their years, their conversations had always been surface level. Politics, neighbors, city problems, work, television. Never did they delve into more serious topics like love, family, kids, health, and death. It just felt wrong. "Stop all this mumbo jumbo."

"No, Tom. Look at me." Richard's voice was more dire than Tom had ever heard it. His eyes looked glassier than usual, but they fixed on his, unwavering. "You're my best friend. And one day, probably soon, I'm going to lose you, and you're going to lose me. Now I don't know if there's a heaven up there, but I sure hope so. I often feel Marlene looking down on me. Maybe I'll get to see you up there, but maybe I won't. We're old. We've lived. I've got nothing left. My Marlene's gone. And I don't have children. Christie will go wherever there's food. And as much as I love seeing your ugly face, a person can only take it for so long. So, knowing my time with you is almost up, I refuse to go without Noel and those kids knowing the truth. If not for your sake, then for Holly's."

Tom pursed his lips. Richard was pushing every button in the arsenal. Death, Noel, Marlene, Holly. He turned toward the door. "You get some rest. I'll make sure Christie is taken care of." Tom patted Richard's hand, feeling the cold, weak skin twitch under his. He cast one more quick glance at Richard, noticing his eyes welling up, and then turned and walked out the door.

CHAPTER 16

WEDNESDAY, DECEMBER 16

Noel had been working nearly nonstop, taking any shift she could to save up enough to afford a place to live. She'd even been searching for apartments in the spare time she had between working, taking the kids to school, cooking, cleaning, and trying to get enough sleep to do it all over again. But the options in town were scarce, and with eight days left, the deal Noel had made with Tom was catching up to her fast.

Then there was the matter of Christmas. The kids had been through so much already, and the last thing they needed was for Santa to forget about them. No, she knew she couldn't let that happen, and she knew she also couldn't just give up on an apartment. These stresses made her miss Bryan more and more with each passing day. Yes, he'd been drinking a lot during the last few weeks of their relationship, but he was still a good man. He'd taken care of the kids with her, and he'd never let her stress about a roof over their heads, or food on the table. Last Christmas, he'd even handed Noel his credit card to make sure the kids had a special Christmas after so much had happened, losing their father and grandmother and moving from city to city and school to school so many times.

Maybe she was looking at it through rose-colored glasses, but she missed him. Noel wanted someone by her side at night, helping her get through the mundane stresses of this thing called life.

After dropping the kids off at school, she parked in front of Glenn Hills Classic Coffee. A light mist hung in the air, giving the town that

Christmassy feel she loved so much. Wreaths hung on the doors of all the shops and businesses. Red ribbons were wrapped around each tree. Lights were strung along branches and windows. People were already walking the sidewalks in their coats, beanies, and scarves, mingling and smiling, shopping for the ones they loved.

Noel drew her lips into a warm smile as she walked through the door to the strong aroma of mocha and vanilla cookies baking in the oven.

"Good morning," Tate said from behind the counter.

"Good morning to you too," she said cheerily.

"You've got a visitor."

Noel turned in surprise. "Really? Who?"

Tate gestured to the table behind her.

She looked over and saw Tom sitting with the pages of a newspaper open in front of him. Tom set the newspaper down when Noel muttered his name in her surprise.

"Humph."

"I'll let you two be," Tate interrupted. "I'll be in the back if you need me."

Noel's gaze didn't leave Tom though. It had suddenly clicked why he was here, and a wave of anger surged through her veins. She looked over her shoulder to ensure Tate was out of earshot, then turned back to Tom. "Are you kidding me?" she whispered, incredulous. "You came down here to ask my boss to vote for you, didn't you? Do you have any idea how bad that makes me look?"

Tom simply watched and waited, silent until she was through. "That's not why I came."

Noel looked at him, his tousled graying hair, scruffy unshaven face, beat-up old blue flannel. He normally looked disheveled, but he looked worse today. Thinking about it, she didn't remember seeing him the night before. The kids had been spying through the window watching the Christmas onlookers come and go, as they usually did with Tom, but he'd been nowhere to be found. "Tom, what's wrong?"

Tom folded his newspaper and took a seat on a barstool at the counter away from the other patrons. "I can't just come to talk?"

Noel stared at him. Tom had come to talk? Was he serious? No, her first suspicions had to be right. Tom must have been there to get to Tate about the Christmas Cup Competition. She decided to test him. "Okay, what do you want to talk about then?"

Tom shrugged. "I just wanted to see how things were going. And I wanted to see the place you've been spending so much time at."

Noel narrowed her eyes, continuing to watch him, gauging his motives. "All right, I suppose. I'll be out by the twenty-fourth, if that's what you're getting at."

"I'm not here to talk about that," Tom insisted. "How do you think the kids are adjusting?"

Noel resisted a scoff. "Really? You're asking about the kids?"

"Yeah, I am."

She took another moment to consider her answer before replying. "They're doing okay. Brittany and Evan seem to like their new school, and they've been loving their walks with Christie. Trevor actually seems happier. Maybe it has something to do with all that decorating you guys have been doing together."

Tom nodded. "He's a good kid. Just a rough exterior."

"Yeah. I suppose I'm to blame for that. He hasn't had it easy. What with moving so many times and then introducing Bryan into his life—" Noel stopped herself. Was she really opening up to Tom? What was happening here?

"No one could have expected what happened to Jacob," Tom said.

Noel tilted her head. This was the most her father had spoken to her since her return. She was sure there was some sort of motive she couldn't yet see. But the man in front of her reminded her of the man that'd been there for her in all those years before her mother's death. Why couldn't he have just admitted what really happened to Holly two years ago? Maybe they wouldn't have fallen out like they had, and maybe then she'd have her dad back.

"I could have made him go to the doctor sooner. I didn't realize cancer could happen so young. I was naive. Jacob even asked me about some of the moles, and I brushed them off as nothing. By the time we found out it was melanoma, it had spread into the lymph nodes."

"You didn't give him the cancer," Tom said, his expression soft.

Noel looked up, suppressing the tears forming in her eyes. "Those kids have put up with so much. I've been so focused on myself for all these years that they got lost in the mix. I'm even sorry that I pushed away from you and Mom. I just wanted to find a way to deal with things on my own. And then I thought maybe all of us would cope better if we found a replacement." A tear fell from her right eye. "Maybe the kids were young enough to think it'd be normal if another man just swooped into their lives, picking up where Jacob left off. Evan had just been born, and Brittany wasn't much older."

Tom stiffened. "Was Bryan bad to you?"

"No. Of course not." Noel inhaled a deep breath. "Is that why you came? You wanted to hear the truth about Bryan?"

He loosened. "No. I barely knew the guy. If you left him, I'm sure he had it coming."

Noel waited before replying, letting the memories flood back in. "He was the one who filed for a divorce. Said he couldn't live up to the man I wanted him to be. Same with the kids—he couldn't be their father. He'd started drinking, so it's probably for the best, but I miss him."

"Doesn't sound like the right man to me. Drinking around the kids isn't all right."

Noel shrugged. She wanted to come to Bryan's defense and explain that it wasn't his fault, but there wasn't any need. He was gone. Tom had a point too, even if he was biased. He'd always been quick to judge, and usually there wasn't much chance of changing his mind.

Tom looked down. He appeared nervous, like he was contemplating saying something.

"What is it?"

He looked up. "Richard's in the hospital."

Noel's eyes went wide. "What? What happened? Is he okay?"

"Yesterday at breakfast, he had a stroke. He's fine now. But he'll be in there a few days. Doctors don't know why it happened."

"Oh, my gosh. I'm so sorry. I can't believe you didn't tell me. What can I do? Can I take him food?"

"I didn't want to worry you or the kids. No. The hospital does that stuff. But Christie will need some taking care of. Went by last night to walk her."

"Of course. I'm sure the kids will be happy to help."

Tom waited, clearly hesitant about replying. After a moment, he finally did. "Do you think that's a good idea?"

"What do you mean?"

Tom huffed out a deep sigh. "The kids are getting attached. They keep talking about wanting a dog for Christmas now."

Suddenly, the realization of what Tom was getting at sank in. He was worried that spending time with the dog would make them want one. And obviously he knew that wasn't a possibility, for an assortment of reasons. "Richard needs our help. The kids are my problem. I'll make sure they know we can't afford a dog right now."

Tom still looked down. "You have enough money for . . . you know, Christmas?"

Why was Tom asking these questions? Did he actually care? "Yeah. I'll handle it. Like I said, we'll be out by the twenty-fourth. You have my word."

Tom opened his mouth as though he were about to say something but stopped himself and nodded. "Good."

Suddenly, the door sprang open, and an older man in a green rain jacket walked in. He smiled at Noel and walked toward the counter.

"I better get back to work," Noel said to Tom, turning toward the customer and putting on a smile.

"How about one of those gingerbread lattes?" the man said pleasantly as Tom nodded again, grabbed his newspaper, and headed out.

"Good choice on a day like today," Noel said. "What size can I get you?"

"A medium will be plenty."

"Great. I'll get that right up for you." Noel moved toward the tablet to ring him up.

Out of the corner of her eye, she watched Tom hobble through the door in his beat-up old flannel and jeans. Part of her felt bad, seeing him leave like that. She supposed he could have stayed longer, and they could have kept talking after the customer was done. He looked sad and lonely. And something had clearly given him a change of heart, what with his coming down to the coffee shop to talk. Probably Richard, Tom's partner in crime. Noel hoped he was all right. Richard was truly one of a kind, a man who could bring a smile to anyone's face with his million-dollar sense of humor. Seeing him have a stroke also had to be tough on Tom.

A strange weight felt lifted from inside her as she watched Tom turn the corner, one that she couldn't explain, but she guessed it meant she was finally turning a new page with her father.

CHAPTER 17

THURSDAY, DECEMBER 17

"How big will the tree be?" Brittany asked from the back seat.

"We'll see," Noel said, glancing over to Tom, who was silently sitting in the passenger seat of the minivan, eyes focused on the road ahead. "It's Tom's house, so whatever he says goes."

She'd been as surprised as anyone when Tom had asked if they'd like to get a tree that evening. He'd insisted it was for their window, to add to the Christmas light display. Noel wasn't so sure, but she wasn't going to be the one to protest. A tree would certainly add to the holiday spirit the kids so desperately needed.

They arrived at Bert's Tree Lot shortly after. Dozens of families, bundled up in their winter wear, frolicked through the sawdust-covered lot filled with trees of all shapes, sizes, and colors: skinny, tall, short, Charlie Brown sparse, silver-dusted, full Douglas firs, spruces, you name it. The kids jumped out of the minivan and immediately took off toward the aisle of Douglas firs. "Santa Claus is Coming to Town" played over a speaker, adding an extra dash of Christmas spirit to the evening.

"Can we get this one, Mom?" Evan shouted, pointing to a tree that had to be nearly ten feet tall.

Noel leaned in to look for the price and nearly did a double take when she saw the one-hundred-fifty-dollar price tag. Of course the kids would go after the largest and most expensive one. She felt Tom's apprehension and regret for deciding to come without even looking at him. "Let's try for a tree that will fit inside the house," she suggested.

The kids skipped along through the rows of trees while Noel and Tom walked side by side at a much more leisurely pace behind them.

Tom stayed silent and expressionless as they went along.

Noel couldn't help but think back to the days when she, Tom, and Holly would come to Bert's Tree Lot, back before Bert had turned it over to his sons. Holly would walk the rows, carefully examining each and every tree. If even a single branch was crooked, she'd pass it up. She'd wish every person in sight a Merry Christmas and would eventually make her way up to Bert himself to thank him for such a beautiful display, to which Bert would always offer her a discount. Noel and Tom would sit back and watch as year after year, Holly picked the perfect tree and got it for an incredible price. As a shy teen, Noel had always admired her mom for it, and hoped someday she'd be able to make nice with others the way Holly did with literally everybody. It wasn't until Noel had met Jacob that she'd started to feel that might be possible.

The kids bounced from one tree to the next, asking for approval. Noel told them no. Tom shook his head. The majority of the rejections came from the fact that the trees were severely out of budget. After three more rows of rejections, they came to a half-off aisle and Tom perked up.

"These ones are ugly," Brittany said, skipping past them.

"Brittany, manners."

Tom moved closer to observe a six-foot-tall Douglas fir. It looked full and lush, but when he pulled it out for a better look, Noel noticed patches missing all over the backside, and a twenty-dollar price tag. Of course Tom would be attracted to the cheapest one in the lot while the kids would be drawn to the most expensive. But if this was the one Tom wanted, she wasn't going to complain. Half a tree was better than no tree at all, and she certainly couldn't afford one of the perfectly shaped ones.

"That one?" Trevor asked, obviously not the one he'd had in mind either.

"What's wrong with it?" Tom croaked.

Trevor sighed. "The back half is almost completely gone."

"Good thing all we need is the front."

"Well, I like it," Evan chirped, reaching up to touch a branch.

"If Evan approves, then it looks like we found the winner," Tom announced, and without waiting for anyone to contest his decision, he gladly carried it to the front to pay and trim the bottom.

Noel thought she'd noticed Tom stumble a bit on his right leg along the way, but when he quickly counterbalanced, she figured it must have been a rock he'd stepped on or something. After paying, however, Tom must have set his pride aside because he actually let one of the workers strap it to the roof of the minivan. Back in the day, when Tom, Noel, and Holly would find a tree together, Tom would never have even entertained the thought of letting someone else strap a tree to the roof of their vehicle. He'd always rambled on about safety precautions and angles. All sorts of nonsense Noel simply ignored.

Thinking about her once-able father and seeing him like this now left Noel feeling nostalgic for what once was and sad for how quickly the time had gone by to get to this point.

The kids buckled up in the back seat, each smiling warmly, excited to get home for the fun part: decorating.

Noel excused herself to the garage to search for the ornaments while Tom and Trevor fiddled with the tree and the stand.

She flipped on the light to the empty garage, and for a second, she'd expected to see her mom's old Honda parked inside. But the moment vanished as the memory of the accident rushed in. She tried to push it away, looking across the garage to the rows of cabinets filled with dozens of cardboard boxes, each marked in Holly's handwriting.

Noel approached the boxes, letting her eyes drift through the labels. Clothes, recipes, salt and pepper shakers—Holly had an obsession with collecting them—tax documents, fine china, Easter, Halloween, and finally, Christmas ornaments. Noel stood there for a long moment, staring at the letters, the slanted cursive she'd seen her mom use time and time again. Then she glanced back over the other boxes filled with all sorts of things Holly had carefully stored inside. Years and years of Holly's things, each still perfectly arranged to come back to at a later date.

Just like her father, Noel had found it best to cope by pushing away the memories as best as she could, but in this moment, they were too difficult to ignore. They came flooding in, each one stabbing her in the heart harder than the next.

The dinners Holly asked Noel to help with so that she, too, could learn to cook like a pro one day. Meatloaf, potato cheese soup, broccoli and chips casserole, peach cobbler, and oh so many more. Halloweens when Holly and Noel would pass out candy to the children together. The antique shops Holly would bring Noel along to in order to find the perfect salt and pepper shakers. And the little moments. Drives home from school. Doing dishes together. Strolls through downtown Glenn Hills. Her mom, the Glenn Hills woman famous for her ribbon-curled blonde perm, her sundresses, and her ability to always know just what to say to anyone at any time.

After a few moments, Noel let out a deep exhale, wiped away her tears, and grabbed the box of ornaments. She stopped to glance once more over the empty garage before crossing through the doorway and reaching back to turn out the lights.

By that point, Tom's face had grown cherry red from exertion, but the tree looked straight. Noel noticed straightaway that while the front looked full, thick, and lush, the backside did indeed appear patchy and sparse, just as it had at the lot. Maybe Tom had been truthful when he said he only cared about getting the tree for the Christmas Cup Competition. Figures.

The little kids started jumping up and down with excitement, seeing the box of ornaments in Noel's hands. Noel noticed the line of cars parked outside, with dozens of families making their way along the sidewalk, taking in the light show and movie. The crowds they were drawing were undoubtedly large, but miniscule in comparison to what she'd seen at the Garcettis' house. Noel shrugged the thought away, opened the box, and then she, Tom, and the kids got to work on decorating the tree.

They pulled out bulbs and ornaments Noel recognized from her childhood. Some from places they'd traveled to, like Las Vegas, New York, and Seattle. Some with baseball team logos. Some with ballerinas, nutcrackers, and Santas. Like an assembly line, Noel took them from the box, and handed them to Tom who handed them to the kids while pointing out the branches that'd work best. Brittany and Evan worked the lower branches, while Trevor worked the top. For a moment, Noel felt like everything was perfect. Tom, Brittany, Evan, Trevor, all working together in harmony, decorating a beautiful Christmas tree, warm inside the house she'd grown up in, with dozens of merry Christmas onlookers just outside, enjoying the Christmas spirit that Tom and Trevor had worked hard to display.

Then it happened. Inside the box, Noel noticed the glass bulb she'd seen so many times over. On the red bulb, in white letters, were the words, *"Will you marry me?"*

Noel contemplated setting it back inside, knowing Tom probably wouldn't be keen on facing the memories the ornament brought with it, but before she knew what was happening, Tom reached over and grabbed the bulb out of her hands. She started to say something, to warn him, but the words caught in her throat.

As though in slow motion, Noel watched as Tom stretched his hand toward Brittany. Suddenly, his gaze drifted down to the bulb, and he hesitated, clearly realizing what it was.

"Will you marry me?" Brittany asked, curious. She reached out, as she'd done with all the other ornaments, grabbed onto the top, and took it.

Tom's hand shook slightly, causing Brittany's fingers to let go.

The bulb flew through the air, and each of them watched as it fell toward the floor. It shattered on impact, spewing shards of glass all over the thin tan carpet. The ornament Tom had used to propose to Holly was gone.

For the longest of moments, all anyone could do was stare.

Brittany's hands shot to her face to cover her eyes, and she burst into tears. "I'm sorry!"

Trevor and Evan watched, wide-eyed, ready for Tom to explode and for Brittany to be sent to time-out.

Tom's eyes stayed glued to the bulb's remnants.

"Maybe we can glue it back together," Noel offered, even though she knew darn well there wasn't any chance of salvaging it from the hundreds of tiny shards.

Tom looked up, his expression stone-faced. "It's okay," he said simply. He stood and then exited the room.

Brittany continued to cry while Trevor and Evan stared.

"It's okay, honey," Noel said, walking over and pulling her in for a hug. "It was just an accident."

Tom emerged from the other room a moment later, an enormous old vacuum in hand.

"Here, Tom, please, let me."

"It's okay. I've got it," he said sternly, looking down, and then he bent over to begin vacuuming the shards.

Noel and the kids watched, unsure of what to say or do.

Tom looked up when Brittany continued crying. "It's okay, Brittany. It was an accident. It's just an ornament."

Noel knew it wasn't just an ornament, and she was pretty sure the kids understood that as well. Nevertheless, Brittany perked up.

"Really?" she asked through harsh sobs.

Tom nodded, his face even redder than when he'd brought the tree inside.

Noel considered kneeling down to help him but decided it wasn't her place. The ornament breaking had been enough, and she didn't want to do anything else to aggravate him worse.

Tom set the vacuum to the side once he'd finished up, then he looked down at Brittany.

"Have you heard the story of that ornament before?" Tom asked.

Noel tilted her head back. She wasn't sure she'd heard him correctly. He wouldn't actually tell her the story, would he? The Tom she knew would never open up the floodgates to such bittersweet memories.

Brittany shook her head.

"Well, let me start with our freshman year of high school. I was telling Trevor the other day how I wasn't a smart student like your mother or grandmother."

Noel flushed when Tom quickly glanced at her. Tom was complimenting her now? What was happening to the Tom she thought she knew? Why was this Tom decorating for Christmas, buying a Christmas tree, shrugging off broken ornaments, and complimenting her? Was he okay? Was it Richard's stroke that had gotten to him?

"Holly was tutoring me, and she told me that if I got an A, she'd go on a date with me," he continued. "She knew I liked her, and she also had no other options. See, I was making her look bad, and your grandmother didn't like looking bad. That was her—everyone had to like her. Anyway, I got that A, and weeks went by without even a mention of the date. So finally, I brought it up one day after school."

The kids waited anxiously to hear what happened next.

Noel had heard the story many times from her mother over the years, especially around Christmastime, but never from her father. Listening to the events recounted from Tom's perspective felt as though she, like the kids, was hearing the story for the first time as well.

"Well, turns out she'd definitely remembered the deal and told me that we would indeed go on a date, but that I'd have to wait until winter break. She said something about having to focus on her studies until then. I remember trying to argue it because we were in October, but she stayed determined, so I waited, my patience wearing a little thinner with each passing day. Finally, two months later, on the last day before winter break, she told me to pick her up that Saturday to take her to the Williamson Christmas Festival."

"Where's Williamson?" Trevor asked.

"Oregon. That's where we both grew up."

"I never knew that," Trevor responded with surprise.

Tom nodded. "Yup. Anyway, that Saturday my mom dropped me off at her house, and I knocked on Holly's door wearing my nicest suit, which in those days wasn't so nice. My mom worked three jobs to get by back then, and my father wasn't around, so we weren't exactly rich. Holly answered the door wearing a red dress and jacket, and I remember thinking she was the prettiest girl I'd ever seen. We walked downtown to the Christmas Festival, and the entire city was there. Back in those days, your grandmother was a popular girl, and I . . . well, let's just say I wasn't. So when a group of her friends called her over, I figured she'd planned to ditch me."

"Did she, Grandpa?" Brittany asked, her eyes shining with curiosity, her tears now gone.

"Nope. She told them she was on a date, and she grabbed my hand. I remember smiling bigger than I'd ever smiled before. We strolled through the park, looking at the giant Christmas trees decorated from head to toe, but neither of us spoke a word. When we got to the end, she pointed up at something in one of the trees above us. And when I looked up, I saw the mistletoe. Or what I thought was mistletoe."

"What's mistletoe?" Evan asked, his face scrunched in confusion.

Tom looked to Noel.

Noel didn't hesitate to step in and answer. "It's a Christmas plant people put up around the holidays. If you get caught standing underneath it with someone, you're supposed to give them a kiss."

"Eww," Evan and Brittany said in unison, and then they burst into giggles.

Trevor blushed.

"Well, anyway," Tom continued, "I got all nervous and embarrassed, and I almost pretended I hadn't seen it. I figured a girl as pretty as Holly wouldn't be caught in a million years kissing a guy like me. But when I looked back down, she leaned in, and suddenly our eyes closed, and then we kissed."

"Eww!" Evan shouted, giggling even harder.

Noel smiled. Tom laughed. "Yup. We kept walking around, enjoying the Christmas music, trees, and lights, all while holding hands. It wasn't until a while afterward that she told me it hadn't actually been mistletoe we'd stood under, but rather holly. She told me about the common misconception and that a lot of people actually hung the wrong plant as a tradition, and that white berries meant mistletoe, red berries meant holly. It was something she took great pride in knowing, since her parents had named her after the plant, after all. I asked her why she'd still kissed me if she'd known it wasn't mistletoe, and she told me that just because it wasn't the right plant didn't mean she didn't want to kiss me. Boy did I smile at that. When it came time to walk her back to her house, I asked her if she'd like to go out again sometime. She told me she would, but not until the next Christmas. I remember laughing, thinking she was joking, but your grandmother was serious. She said that school was starting again, that she'd need to focus, and that she spent summers in New York visiting her grandparents. Then school would start again, and the next time she'd be able to do another date wouldn't be until the following Christmas. And just like that, my happiness deflated. I saw her almost every day the rest of the school year and even after summer the next school year. We talked from time to time, but mostly just quick greetings. I figured that Christmas would come and she'd forget all about the promise she'd made."

Noel glanced over at each of the kids and found each of their eyes glued to Tom. She had to admit he had a way with storytelling, and even though she already knew what would happen, she too wanted to hear what came next.

Tom continued. "The whole month of December passed without even a mention of it, but then, on the last day before break, she told me to pick her up that Saturday to take her to the Williamson Christmas

Festival again. I couldn't believe it at first, but I wasn't going to pass it up. That Saturday, I wore the same suit, granted I'd grown and it didn't fit the same, but my mom couldn't afford to get me a new one in those days. Holly came out wearing a beautiful green Christmas dress, with pigtails, and again, I remember thinking she was the most beautiful girl I'd ever seen. She held my hand the entire time, and when we got to the end to the holly that was supposed to be mistletoe, she pulled me in to kiss me, and I knew I was in trouble."

"Why were you in trouble?" Brittany tilted her head, confused.

Tom laughed. "I loved her."

Brittany smiled, a look of understanding dawning in her eyes.

"But it happened again. When I asked her if we could date during the year, she told me not until the next Christmas. I couldn't believe it. I knew she liked me back, but she didn't change her mind. I was worried that maybe another guy would swoop her up during the year. The next year came and went pretty quickly, and sure enough, several guys tried to fight for her attention, each asking her out. But from what I'd heard around school, she had turned them all down. The last day before Christmas break came again, and she found me and told me to pick her up for Christmas. We went to the same park. I got smart this time though. I knew I would have her for only a couple of hours until I'd have to wait until the next year, so I asked her if we were going to do this forever, just once a year."

"And what'd she say?" Trevor asked, completely enthralled.

"She said yes. But that didn't stop us from talking each day leading up to it. We kissed under the holly that was supposed to be mistletoe again, and I walked her home. When school started up again, I didn't waste any time. I asked her to eat lunch with me, and to my surprise, she agreed.

"Eventually I started asking her to tutor me again after school, and she agreed. Soon, I even convinced the principal to let me change my schedule to the same as hers because I was doing much better in the classes she was in. I even started going to the same church as she did, and instead of seeing her two times a week with tutoring, it grew to seeing her several hours each day. During the year, we never held hands, hugged, or kissed. Soon, our senior year started, and Holly started talking about going off to college in California. Without telling her, I applied to the same schools. Then, right before winter break, she got the news that she'd gotten into UCLA. Then I got my own envelope from UCLA."

"Did you get in?" Trevor interrupted.

Tom shook his head. "Nope. And I knew that she'd go away to California, start school, and forget about me and Williamson."

"So what did you do?" Brittany asked.

"Well, our yearly Christmas Eve date at the Williamson Christmas Festival came around again, and I decided I had to do something big because if I didn't, I might not ever get another date. I arrived at the park early to set it up. Then I picked her up that evening, and we walked through the rows of Christmas trees, holding hands, and talking just like we always did. Again, I remember thinking she was the most beautiful girl in the world. She was wearing a silver dress and had her hair curled. She laughed the whole way through, smiling every second of the way. Then we got to the end where the holly usually hung, and she didn't even look up, just pulled me in for a kiss. Almost made me pass out, as long as it took me to come up for air. After we kissed, I asked her what the kiss was for. She looked at me, confused. When I pointed up, showing her there wasn't any mistletoe or holly, her eyes went wide. Hanging above us was an ornament my mother helped me make, with the words, 'Will you marry me?' etched across it. My mom knew how much I loved her and had actually been the one to tell me that if I didn't want to lose her, then I had to do something about it. Holly stared for what felt like days, before finally looking down. When she did, I was on one knee, with a ring in my hands. I'd spent all year working odd jobs saving up enough for it. One hundred dollars, the most expensive thing I'd ever bought in my entire life."

"What'd she say?" Evan shouted.

"I told her that I couldn't live without her, and that I couldn't let her move to L.A., where she'd disappear for the rest of my life. I told her I'd come with her, that I'd find work and help support her through it. I must have been waiting on my knee for half an hour until finally, she said yes. We got married the next Christmas."

All three kids smiled from ear to ear. Noel did too.

It was one of the most romantic stories Noel had ever heard, and her father, of all people, had been the one to make it happen. Why couldn't she have a romance as special as Tom and Holly's? Why had she always been dealt the bad hand when it came to romance? Jacob, her perfect man, ripped from her life far too young. Or Bryan, the one that had almost seemed like the perfect replacement for Jacob, until he'd suddenly changed his mind.

For a second, an image of the scruffy, always-smiling Tate popped into her head. Her boss, the only one who'd taken a chance on her because he appreciated the hard work that came with being a mother. But he was also guarded, and thinking about it, she didn't even really know much about him other than the fact that he was a widower.

Noel pushed the thought away, refocusing on the present moment with Trevor, Evan, Brittany, and Tom, sitting around the newly decorated tree with cheerful onlookers just outside, enjoying the spirit and magic of Christmas. Tom and the kids continued to place ornaments throughout the tree for the onlookers outside to see. Noel watched Tom as he handed a clear glass angel to Brittany.

What was happening to him? Spending time decorating for Christmas with his family? Telling the story of how he and Holly had come to be? Embracing his family and feelings more than he had in years. Tom, the man who'd become a brick wall after Holly's death, and who still wouldn't tell Noel what really happened that night. The man who'd closed himself off from the world completely. Something had changed him, and Noel didn't yet know what it was. But she intended to find out.

CHAPTER 18

FRIDAY, DECEMBER 18

Tom hobbled out to the mailbox under the hazy gray late-afternoon sky. His right leg had recently been going numb far more often than he cared to admit, and he still hadn't gone back to the doctor. He knew that the doctor would simply take his blood pressure and blood sugar, then tell him to cut sugar and walk more, same as always.

"Afternoon, Tom," called a woman from across the street.

Tom looked up as he pulled the envelopes from the mailbox. An older plump, graying woman wearing a red sweat suit stood holding the leash to a giant Great Dane. He was certain he didn't know her, but he replied curtly as she began to cross the street. "Afternoon."

He looked back at his mail and noticed an envelope with the words, "Northern California Electric," printed in bold along the front. It was the bill he'd been waiting for. He slid his finger along the corners, then ripped the top open.

"Getting ready to turn the Christmas lights on soon?"

Tom glanced up again. It was the same woman standing just a few feet away. What the heck did she want? And who was she anyway?

Tom nodded, expressionless.

The woman leaned in closer, after looking over her shoulder, and then she whispered, "I hear the judges are looking mighty hard at your house this year. There's talk that maybe it's time for a new winner for the Christmas Cup."

"Oh?" Tom asked.

The woman shrugged. "You didn't hear it from me, but I hope you win. Your house really is beautiful. My grandkids love it. We'll be rooting for you at the winner's ceremony on the twenty-second."

Tom stood, thinking about her words. Could the judges really choose them over the Garcettis? The Garcettis had had an ice rink, for crying out loud. "Thanks," he finally said.

The woman winked and continued on down the street with her dog.

Tom watched them for a moment, considering it some more, then looked back down at the letter he'd opened. He pried out the paper from inside, and unfolded it.

Northern California Electric. Amount Due: $338.97.

Oh boy. The price was over triple his usual hundred-dollar electric bill. He'd had a feeling that with Noel and the kids, his expenses would increase. Living on a fixed budget, Tom had outlined every expense each month, and always had fifty dollars left. That was it, no more, no less. He usually spent it on extra sweets at the grocery store. This month he'd spent his extra money on Christmas lights and a Christmas tree, and last he checked, he had sixty-two dollars in his bank account. The electric bill was only for half the month, but already, Tom knew the Christmas lights wouldn't be cheap. He also knew that he didn't have the money. If they won the Christmas Cup Competition, it wouldn't be an issue, but he couldn't count on that. Just because a neighbor thought she'd heard rumors that the judges were considering his house didn't make it fact. So what was he supposed to do? Ask Noel? Turn the lights off?

"Hi, Grandpa!" Brittany called.

He looked over the brick wall to Richard's house. Brittany and Evan were holding Christie's leash. Christie's tail was wagging like crazy, and her tongue was hanging out the side of her mouth. Richard was still in the hospital, and Tom hadn't gone back. After the way things ended with their last conversation, Tom didn't want to go anyway. Richard needed to mind his own business. It wasn't Richard's secret to tell, so the old blabbermouth had better keep his mouth shut.

Tom waved back.

The kids ran in circles, laughing and smiling as Christie chased them. Tom could tell they really enjoyed living here. Walking Christie, their new school, their teachers, the Christmas lights, the Christmas Cup Competition, everything. They'd always been young moving from one house to the next. So being in a new house must have felt normal to them, and Tom guessed they hadn't really given much thought to it. Then there was Trevor.

He, too, seemed to be warming up to Glenn Hills and the house, but Trevor, unlike the other two, was old enough to know that their situation wasn't normal. He'd switched schools, made and lost friends, and had a man in his life trying to replace his father. Tom could tell that Trevor had become numb to it, like Tom had, putting up a wall to block out the feelings. Except for maybe his crush on that girl, Kayla. He could also tell that the boy really liked working on the Christmas lights, and that Trevor really wanted to win the competition. If they didn't win, it would be yet another thing in his life that hadn't gone his way. Trevor didn't need that; he'd already been dealt a rough enough hand.

Tom knew he couldn't turn off the Christmas lights. The kids needed them too much at that moment. He'd have to find another way to come up with the money. The best solution he could think of right then was that he needed to find a way to win.

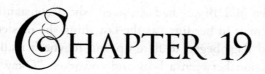

CHAPTER 19

SATURDAY, DECEMBER 19

Noel finished drying off the mugs and wiped her hands on her apron. Outside the shop, people of all sorts began gathering downtown for the annual Glenn Hills Christmas Stroll. There, local artists presented their Christmas displays, the school hosted a wreath-decorating booth for the kids, the city provided hot cocoa and apple cider, the local church displayed a live nativity scene, and Santa came for children to tell him their Christmas wishes. Noel remembered Holly taking her every year, always working with her to decorate a new wreath for the door. Usually Tom would come along too, in more of a supervisory role than anything else.

"Almost done?" Tate asked, standing in the doorway.

"Yes, sir. Ready to close up?"

Tate lifted a brow. "*Sir*? Come on, I'm not that old, am I?"

Noel shrugged, and they both broke into smiles. She took off her apron and followed Tate to the door to lock up for the night as they usually did. But then he turned around to meet her eyes. She waited, looking up at him curiously.

"Hey, would you like to check out the Christmas Stroll with me?"

Noel's head bobbed back slightly as she tried to process the unexpected request. Was he asking her on a date? Or was it a casual interaction between a boss and his employee?

Tate seemed to notice her hesitancy and butted in. "Sorry. If you have plans or need to get home, I understand. I just thought it might be fun. I've never been."

Noel narrowed her eyes. She was usually pretty good at recognizing when men were flirting with her, and now her radar was going crazy. Part of her wanted him to be asking her out, but part of her was resistant. Since she and Bryan had divorced, she'd constantly reminded herself that a man in her life was the last thing she needed right now. Dozens of red flags began to flare up, but maybe it really was just a simple interaction between a boss and coworker. "Okay. I suppose I could join you for a bit."

"Great." Tate smiled confidently and opened the door for Noel.

"Thank you."

While Tate quickly locked up, Noel looked over to the windshield of a car parked in front of the coffee shop. She caught a glance of herself, a strand of her hair hanging over her forehead. She quickly pulled it back into her high pony and then smiled to make sure her makeup still looked all right. Her lips could use some color, but other than that, she supposed she looked okay. At least as good as a broke, recently divorced mom of three could look.

"Ready?" Tate asked. Noel turned around, hoping Tate hadn't caught her checking herself out. "Get a good look?"

"At what?" she asked, playing coy.

"That pretty woman in the reflection."

Noel blushed hard. Was she wrong, or was he flirting? She struggled for a second to find the words. "Just had to make sure my hair looked decent."

"And it does. How's mine?" He leaned in toward his own reflection and ran an exaggerated hand through perfectly slicked brown hair.

Noel hit him lightly on the shoulder. "Oh, stop it."

Tate finished pretend-fixing his hair and then straightened up and looked down to meet Noel's eyes again. "Shall we?" he asked, gesturing toward the crowd of people making their way toward their intended destination.

"We shall."

They strode off down the sidewalk, past the shops and restaurants all closed up for the evening's festivities. Walking by Tate's side, Noel noticed he was taller than she'd realized, and also bigger. Of course she hadn't missed that he was a strong-looking man, but something in the way he carried himself while he walked made him look even stronger. Again, Noel pushed the thought away. She needed to stop sizing him up. They were simply checking out the Christmas Stroll as coworkers, nothing more.

A sign reading *North Pole* marked the start of the Stroll grounds, and it was strung between two giant candy cane poles on either side of the street. Kids and families of all sorts bustled around them. On both sides of the streets, the trees were lit from top to bottom with glistening white lights. Red bows were tied around the trunks of each tree. "Deck the Halls" played loud in the background over all the noise of the crowd. A smiling teenage redhead holding a tray of Styrofoam cups approached them.

"Apple cider?" she asked cheerily.

Tate looked down at Noel.

"Sure, thank you," Noel said.

Tate reached over and grabbed a cup for each of them. "Thank you," he added as the girl smiled and walked over to the next group of Stroll goers.

Noel took a cup and brought it to her nose. The steam warmed her face and the strong smell of apples and caramel hung in the air. She took a slow sip, letting the tasty drink tickle her taste buds and soothe her throat.

"Not bad," Tate announced after taking a sip, "but it's got nothing on ours."

"Be nice," Noel teased, smiling up at him.

Night had fallen, and the warm cup in her hands helped to combat the nip in the air. Tate stepped toward a booth on the left where several kids had gathered around. Noel stepped in behind the crowd as well, and they both looked down to the sidewalk where an artist was working on a mural of Santa sitting in a sleigh, drinking a glass-bottled Coke. The detail in Santa's face looked almost as lifelike as a photograph: rosy cheeks, feathered white beard and all.

"Wow," Tate said.

Noel nodded, impressed. The artist was a short, long-haired boy who couldn't have been any more than fifteen years old. They watched him rub his fingers along the sleigh, etching out the brown, giving the wood an aged, faded look. Then they continued along, sipping on their caramel apple ciders while checking out the other art displays: A Christmas tree made from recycled CDs. A toy soldier ice sculpture. Another chalk art piece, but this one an abstract take on a snowman, with reds, greens, and whites spread throughout several small circles and squares, coming together to form the snowman's body.

"What am I doing with my life?" Tate asked, looking down at yet another teenage artist working on the snowman.

Noel nodded in agreement. "These kids are very talented."

"Speaking of kids, how's the Christmas Cup Competition coming along? Didn't you say that your kids and father were entering this year? Something about your father wanting you to bribe me?"

"Yeah, that's Tom for you." Noel's face went hot with embarrassment. "The kids have really been enjoying it. They hide behind the windows each night, watching as people park their cars and walk around the yard, taking in the light show and movie. It's been fun."

"Well, I look forward to seeing it," Tate said. "Who knows? Maybe you will win."

"Maybe." Noel shrugged. "The Garcettis' house is pretty special this year, though."

"Yeah, I've heard talk. That's the woman I said I would kick out next time if I had to, right?"

Noel looked up, surprised he remembered. "Yes, it was."

What did it mean if Tate didn't care for Samantha? Was there a chance others didn't as well? Was there actually a chance Tom and Trevor could win? Maybe, but she was getting ahead of herself.

"The other day we were getting to know each other," Tate continued. "I still want to know more about you, Noel VanHansen."

Noel curled her lips into a tight smile. "Oh you do, do you, Mr. Tate?"

Tate laughed, bumping her shoulder playfully.

Noel laughed too, and again, she couldn't help but wonder if he was flirting.

They stopped laughing as they approached a crowd near the end of the street gathered around a stable. Men dressed as the wise men walked out bearing gifts. Several goats and donkeys moved about the stable behind a barbed wire fence. They strode together toward the scene.

"Is it ever lonely for you being back here?" Tate asked. "You said you came because of a messy divorce, and you said your father wanted you out or something, right?"

Great, back to the hard-hitting questions, Noel thought. "You're certainly direct, aren't you?"

Tate shrugged innocently.

"Well, yes. Sometimes it gets lonely. I miss having someone to just talk to at home."

Tate nodded as they stood together at the back of the crowd.

"What about you?" Noel prodded. He had gotten personal with her, after all. "Without your wife, I mean. It must be hard."

Out came a woman dressed as Mary, holding a crying baby swaddled in white blankets. The crowd laughed as Mary opted to set the baby in the manger, the crying part clearly not exactly what she'd signed up for.

Tate let out a soft chuckle, then turned back to Noel.

She wondered if he would dodge the question. Had she gone too far?

"Yes, it's tough at times. I miss Alice. But moving away from Oregon after it happened was good. A fresh start of sorts."

Noel thought about whether or not to press him further. He intrigued her, and she wanted to know him better. Not many people could truly understand what it was like to lose a spouse. "If you don't mind me asking, why Glenn Hills? Of all the places you could have gone, why a small town like this?"

Tate met her eyes. "The truth?"

Noel nodded.

"I couldn't handle it anymore. The entire city knew what had happened, and everyone acted as though it was me that killed her. Everyone thought they knew me, and everyone talked. I needed out of there and told myself I'd move a thousand miles away. So I found a spot on the map that was exactly a thousand miles away. I don't know why, but it just felt right. I packed up, and here I am."

His answer left Noel with more questions than it did answers. She certainly understood what it was like to be the talk of the town because of a death, and the need for getting away, but had he really just picked a place exactly a thousand miles away? And that place happened to be Glenn Hills? What were the chances of that? And what happened to his wife? Knowing from experience how much she herself still hated that question, how hard it was to have to endure the memories while explaining the death of the loved one, Noel decided not to press him on it. She knew that if he wanted her to know, he would tell her.

Joseph walked into the nativity, with the shepherds following behind.

"Mommy!" a girl shouted from behind them.

Noel thought she recognized Brittany's voice. She turned, and then she saw them, Evan and Brittany rocketing toward her.

"Brittany? Evan?" Noel gasped as they clutched onto her waist.

"Hi, Mommy!" Evan screamed. Several of the people looking at the nativity scene glanced over at the commotion.

Trevor approached behind them, wearing all black with his hair spiked straight up as always. Then came Tom wearing an old beat-up tan coat and loose, faded jeans.

"What are you all doing here?" Noel asked, rubbing Evan and Brittany's backs and then reaching over to playfully touch Trevor's spiky hair.

Noel noticed Tate smile wide as he watched her embrace the kids.

"I thought they might want to see the Stroll," Tom grumbled.

Tom's idea? Seriously, what was going on with him? The Christmas Cup Competition was one thing, but the Christmas Stroll too?

"Great," Noel finally said with excitement.

"Hey, Tom, good to see you again," Tate announced, breaking the silence, sticking his hand out for Tom to shake.

Tom nodded and accepted it.

"Who are you?" Evan asked, looking up at him.

Tate laughed. "I'm Tate. I work with your mom at the coffee shop."

Noel smiled, waiting for Evan's response. Evan stared up at him, as though he were studying him. Noel stepped in, pointing to Tate and then pointing to Evan. "Tate, this is Evan, Brittany, Trevor, and Tom, whom you've already met."

Tate gave them each a wave.

Silence lingered on the air for a moment afterward.

"You're big," Evan finally said.

"Thanks. That's a cool sweatshirt," Tate replied, giving Evan a wink.

Noel looked down and saw Evan was wearing the Rudolph the Red-Nosed Reindeer sweatshirt he'd asked for last Christmas.

"It's Rudolph," Evan pointed out.

"He's the best reindeer of them all," Tate replied, to which both Evan and Noel smiled.

"Why is your beard so big?" Brittany asked.

Tate laughed again. "I don't have a pretty face like yours, so I grow my beard out to hide it."

Brittany giggled, and Noel smiled, appreciating the effort he was making to help the kids feel comfortable.

Tate looked over to Trevor. "I hear you and your grandpa have put on quite the display this year. It's the talk of the town."

"Really?" Genuinely surprised, Trevor looked back to Tom to gauge his reaction.

For the slightest of seconds, Noel thought she saw Tom break a smile, but then he returned to his normal stone-faced look. "The Garcettis have an ice rink and a Santa, though."

"Those might be impressive too, but I heard you guys have *It's a Wonderful Life* playing every night," Tate fired back coolly. "That's my favorite Christmas movie."

Trevor grinned. Oh, Tate was good. Getting Trevor to grin was no easy feat, especially lately.

"Well, I guess I should let you all be to enjoy the Stroll as a family," Tate said.

Noel put her arm around Trevor and then looked up. She'd been enjoying their time together, and he'd been so good with her kids and Tom.

"You don't have to go," Tom offered.

"Thanks, Tom, but it's okay. I need to get home anyway. It was great meeting you all," Tate said with a smile. "Thanks for the walk, Noel. I'll see you later." He met her eyes as his hand touched her shoulder, sending tiny shockwaves up her neck. They held each other's gazes for another moment, and then finally he looked away and waved goodbye to the kids.

"Have a good night, Tate," Noel said. He turned back to give her a quick smile before continuing on.

She watched as he walked off into the crowd. In that moment, she knew she'd been right. Tate definitely liked her, and as much as she didn't want to admit it, she liked him too.

"Can we get hot chocolate?" Brittany asked.

"Yeah, can we?" Evan seconded.

"I wouldn't mind one myself," Tom added.

Noel looked down at the kids, then up at Tom, always one with a sweet tooth, just like the kids. "Sure, let's go get some hot chocolate."

CHAPTER 20

SUNDAY, DECEMBER 20

Noel spent most of the day calling about apartments for rent. She'd left a total of eighteen voicemails, and had spoken to three people, all of whom had told her that they wouldn't be available to show their apartments until after Christmas. She only had four more days before her deal with Tom was up. It seemed like Tom was more receptive to their presence now than he'd been when they'd first arrived, but still, she'd made a promise, and she couldn't bring herself to ask Tom for an extension on that promise. Plus, she knew that he'd want them out for Christmas. Even if he'd entered the competition and bought a Christmas tree and taken the kids to the Christmas Stroll, she knew how much he hated the day, and she doubted very much that he'd change his mind about that.

Then there was the matter of Christmas presents: Trevor, dropping subtle hints that he'd like a Playstation, while Evan and Brittany not-so-subtly mentioning they wanted a dog.

Obviously with her budget and living accommodations, neither of those were viable options, but she'd vowed that she'd do her best to make their Christmas special.

First, she needed an apartment.

Noel looked up from her laptop when a knock sounded at the door, and then she gazed out the living room window to find that the sun was setting over the rolling foothills, the sky now a dark purple. Christmas light goers would soon be coming by to see the display. Could one of them be at the door for some reason?

"I got it," Tom grumbled from down the hall.

Evan and Brittany continued to play with a toy train under the Christmas tree, while Trevor worked on some homework he'd received for winter break. Noel looked back down to her laptop as Tom opened the door. She couldn't see anything from behind the wall, but she listened curiously, waiting to hear whomever it might be.

"Hello, sir, is Noel here by chance?"

Noel's eyes shot toward the wall blocking her view of the door, recognizing the voice instantly. Her heart pounded. What was he doing here? She leapt up and moved swiftly toward the door.

"You better have a darn good explanation for why I shouldn't kick you to the curb right this second," Tom said, anger flaring in his voice.

"Tom!" Noel shouted, moving around Tom until Bryan came into view.

"Noel," Bryan said.

"You came back here after what you did to my daughter? You must have a death wish!" Tom lunged through the door toward him.

"Tom!" Noel yelled again, stepping in front of Tom to stop his attack. She could feel Tom's anger as he huffed and puffed, restraining himself. It occurred to her that she couldn't remember a time Tom had ever stood up for her like this, or anyone for that matter. She waited another moment until he cooled down. "It's okay, Tom. I'll take care of it. Why don't you keep an eye on the kids inside?"

Tom kept glaring, his breathing still unsteady. "Fine," he finally said, giving Bryan a long, hard look and then turning to head back inside.

Noel waited until Tom was completely out of sight before shutting the door, then she turned around to face the man with buzzed blonde hair and broad swimmer's shoulders, wearing a suit. "What are you doing here, Bryan?"

He took a step toward her, and Noel backed up.

"I got your messages." Bryan looked at her pleadingly, the same as when he'd gotten down on one knee at the Golden Gate Bridge. "And since you've been gone, I've been doing a lot of thinking."

"Oh you have, have you?"

Bryan nodded. "I miss you, Noel. I know what I did was wrong. All of it." He paused. "I stopped drinking."

Noel stared into his eyes, her head spinning. Part of her wanted to jump into his arms and embrace him. The other part wanted to tell him to get lost because of what he'd done to her and the kids. Yes, she'd missed him. Yes, she'd left him a message on her drive down and another one after the job interview. But in the past week, she'd also taken steps to focus on herself and her children, which meant putting men on the back burner. Especially the man who'd filed for a diorce and asked her to leave with no warning, shattering both her and her kids' lives. She looked back to the house, noticing four sets of eyes spying on them from behind the window.

"You look different," Bryan said, breaking the silence. "In a good way. You look beautiful."

Noel glanced down at her plain white T-shirt and jeans—not exactly the height of fashion. She also hadn't bothered to do her hair or makeup, assuming she'd be spending her Sunday apartment hunting, not seeing her ex-husband.

"What are you doing, Bryan? You come here and try to flatter your way back to me? Is that it? Where were these comments the last couple of months before you kicked us out?"

He moved closer. "Look, I already know what I did was wrong. I don't know what to say. The pressure got to me."

"What pressure?" Noel shot back. "What was so difficult about being with me? You never even gave me an explanation."

Bryan looked down for a long moment and then finally glanced back up to meet Noel's eyes. "The pressure of living up to your standard of Jacob."

"What are you talking about, Bryan?" Noel couldn't remember Bryan ever mentioning him before. Each time Noel brought him up, Bryan usually went quiet.

Bryan sighed. "He's the father of your children. Your first love. The way you talk about him—it's just difficult to live up to. The way he cooked. The way he always knew what to say when you had a bad day. The way he taught Trevor to ride a bike. The way he tucked the kids into bed."

Noel couldn't believe it. Yes, she'd thought about Jacob when Bryan made her mad and couldn't cheer her up, or had done things *differently* than Jacob had, like barbecuing, or reading bedtime stories to the kids, or picking the right gifts for holidays. But had she really talked about him that much? In those subtle ways, she supposed she must have. How could she not? When sharing a life with a partner, you can't help but compare them to previous partners. Especially if a previous partner had been perfect in every way.

She looked up at Bryan, his pleading eyes, his clean-shaven face. He looked different too. The bags under his eyes had disappeared and his bloated red face from the drinking had faded. His belly had also trimmed down. He'd gotten his hair buzzed tighter. He looked good, cleaner—like Jacob.

"I'm sorry," she finally said. "You're right. I did put pressure on you to live up to him, and that wasn't right, but I've got a lot going on now. I have a job. The kids have started new schools. I'm trying to find an apartment. Plus, there's Christmas right around the corner, and I still haven't bought the kids' presents."

"If you come back home, I can take care of all that. No need to find an apartment, and we can buy them presents together. Plus, they've only missed a couple weeks at their old schools. I'm sure they could go back easily."

As he talked, Noel pictured everything he was saying. She and the kids moving back in, acting as though their couple weeks in Glenn Hills had simply been a temporary vacation. The kids going back to their old schools and friends. Their routines. Christmas shopping with Bryan. Not having to worry about having enough for rent, food, and Christmas presents. But what about the life she was starting to build in Glenn Hills? Her job at the coffee shop? Her kids and their new schools? Tom, coming around to the father he'd once been? And Tate? Despite her vow to push men away and focus on her priorities, she'd felt something between them at the Christmas Stroll, and she had a feeling he did too.

"Look," Bryan said. "Why don't you take a little bit to think about it? I'll be staying at the inn downtown. When you're ready to talk, just let me know."

Noel opened her mouth to speak but found she couldn't. He was right; she needed time. She nodded.

He gave her a weak smile, then hesitated a second before stepping in and kissing her on the cheek. The warm, soft touch against her skin brought with it all the memories of their past. Their romantic nights out. Those nights lying in bed, reading books together. Him proposing at the Golden Gate Bridge. Bryan lingered a second; then he walked down the cement pathway back to his car.

Tom stood outside Noel's room, his hand hovering over the doorknob. After seeing Bryan, he'd almost beaten him to a pulp. Well, maybe not a pulp, but the man needed to be taught a lesson. Do something like that to a man's daughter and grandkids, and come back expecting all will be okay? No. Bryan had a lot of nerve, and Tom wouldn't stand for him manipulating his way back into their lives. But it wasn't Tom's decision, as hard as that fact was to bear.

Noel had gone back into the house, and instead of closing herself off, she'd gone to play with the kids on the floor. The sun disappeared, giving way to a cool, dark night, and another evening of Christmas lights and Christmas onlookers. Only two more days until the winner's ceremony at the Town Hall. The crowd outside the house was even bigger than the previous night, with easily three hundred people watching, and the kids ate it all up, hiding behind window sills watching the onlookers in awe.

Tom took a deep breath, and then he finally knocked. He could hear movement inside, but no response, so he tried again.

"Yeah?" Noel called out.

Tom opened the door.

Noel sat up on her bed, closing her laptop. Her eyes were red and puffy.

"I . . . I, uh," Tom sputtered. "Well, I just thought I'd check on you."

Noel let out a light laugh. "Thanks. I'm fine. Just a lot going on."

"Seems like it." Tom lingered in the doorway, contemplating coming inside.

"Are the kids all right?"

Tom nodded. "Oh, yeah. They're fine. The crowd outside is big tonight. They'll be distracted for hours."

Noel laughed again.

Tom had missed her laugh. It was the same throaty laugh as Holly's.

"I think I might take him up on his offer," Noel said, glancing up for Tom's reaction. "Bryan, I mean."

"Oh," Tom said, trying not to let his disappointment show.

"I mean, it's just easier that way. The kids can go back to their old schools and friends. We won't have to worry about finding an apartment, and we'll be able to afford everything again. Food, presents."

"I see." If there was one thing Tom had learned from Holly, it was that telling a woman what to do was never wise. Any time Tom had felt like giving Holly his two cents, she'd typically rebut his ideas, purely as a matter of spite. Holly was always right, and her ideas needed to be just that, *her* ideas. It had taken a while to catch on, but when he finally did, he'd learned much more subtle approaches to getting his opinions out there. "Well, how do you feel things are going here in Glenn Hills?" he asked.

Noel looked toward the window, contemplating it. "Surprisingly, not bad. Hard. But not bad. The kids seem to like it, and my job is actually pretty good. Tate's been great. But living on a single mom's salary isn't easy, and I've only just begun."

Tom nodded. Talking wasn't his strong suit anymore. Maybe it never was, but he had a story to tell, and he knew it wouldn't come easy, because like everything else, anytime he thought of Holly, the feelings it brought back stabbed him straight in the heart. "You know, have I ever told you the story of how I almost left Los Angeles and your mother to go back home to Oregon?"

Noel tilted her head, thinking about it. "No. What story? You almost left Mom?"

"As stupid as it sounds, yes, I did." Tom took a deep breath, letting the memories flood back in as he stepped in to take a seat on the foot of her bed. "It was not long after she started her freshman year of college. We'd gotten married and moved into a little apartment in downtown L.A. I'd started school to be an electrician while working at a burger joint nights and weekends. We were barely scraping by, and Holly was always at school, making new friends, learning all sorts of neat stuff and what have you. It felt like the only times I saw her were right before bed, and the occasional Sunday morning."

Tom paused a moment, picturing Holly coming home from school, smiling from ear to ear, going on about her new friends or her professors. All he'd been able to think about at the time was his own school and work, and how neither of those were as exciting as hers.

"I started to miss my mom. I knew she'd struggled to support me working three jobs all by herself. She must have been struggling without me there to help, even though she wrote me letters that said otherwise. I began to miss my friends. The old bike path and the lake. The great outdoors. I grew to hate the bustle of L.A. I started to wonder if I'd made a mistake."

"I didn't know this," Noel interrupted, her eyebrows pensively furrowed.

"Yup. Not something I liked talking about. Anyway, one week went by during which I'd only spoken to Holly for about a minute. Over that week, I wrote a letter to my mom in secret. Told her how hard it was, and how Holly was off learning and having fun while I was struggling and working like a dog. I wrote how I was thinking about taking the train back home. How I'd move back and become an electrician there."

"So what happened?"

"I got a letter back. My mom's letters usually went on for pages and pages, but this one was only one line. She said, 'What will you give up if you give up? You are the only one who has the chance to find out.'"

Noel raised her eyebrows. "Wow. Wise woman."

"The wisest. I thought about what she'd said all day and night. She was right. I was the only one who'd know what I'd give up, and if I left, I'd never find out.

"I knew that as tough as times were, I wanted to find out. So I told Holly about it, and she was mad at first, but she came around. We ended up setting aside more time for each other, and you know what? Things got easier. I finished school, stopped working at the burger place, and started working as an electrician. Holly made more friends, studied, and even got a job as an accountant. We moved to Glenn Hills, bought the house, and then we had you. None of that would have happened if I'd moved back home."

A tear fell from Noel's eye. She reached over to touch Tom's arm. He looked down at the gesture.

He felt tears welling up in his own eyes, but he kept them back as best as he could. "I'm not saying that going back to him is giving up, but what will you give up if you do? Is it something you want to find out?" Tom got up from the bed; then he took a deep breath. He'd said what he needed to say. "Let me know if you need anything." He turned to walk back out of the door.

"Wait," Noel said.

Tom turned to look at her.

Noel's eyes locked onto his. "Thanks, Dad."

A feeling of warmth rushed through Tom's body. Just for a second, he felt like he was back to the days when his daughter and wife were still with him, happy and healthy, living in their home together. He smiled softly and nodded and walked out the door and down the hall.

CHAPTER 21

MONDAY, DECEMBER 21

Just one more day until the big Christmas Cup Competition winner's announcement. Noel parked the minivan in front of the coffee shop as California's biggest storm in years crept into town just in time for Christmas. A light sprinkle splashed against the windshield, but for some reason, the winter weather didn't leave her with that same Christmas spirit it had just days prior. Instead, the ominous deep-gray sky reflected the confusion and sadness within her.

She hadn't slept all night, thinking about Bryan and his proposition while Evan and Brittany tossed and turned alongside her. She thought about the couple years they'd spent together, and the years they could have in the future. Then there was Glenn Hills, and the newfound hope of unknown possibilities that came with it. A new house. A job. A reborn relationship with her father. A new school for her children. Even the possibility of a new man. Eventually.

She'd also thought about her father's story about nearly leaving her mom and the letter his mom wrote him. *What will you give up if you give up? You are the only one who has the chance to find out.* The question inspired her but also left her torn. Both ways she'd give up something. But with Bryan, at least she wouldn't struggle to support her kids. And maybe she really could be happy with him. Isn't that what she'd wanted all along?

Noel tried to push her dilemma away as she dashed through the light rain and into the shop. Inside, the warm air felt decadent against her cheeks. The smell of fresh ground coffee and cinnamon rolls baking in the oven filled her nostrils.

"Hey there," Tate said from behind the counter, offering her a wide grin.

"Morning, Tate," Noel said, a bit more dryly than she'd anticipated. She made her way around the counter, washed her hands, and then put on her apron.

Tate's smile dimmed as he watched her. "Everything okay?"

Noel averted her eyes toward the oven, where a batch of cinnamon rolls was baking. "Just fine."

Tate continued to stare at her, his expression furrowed in question. "Is this about the other night? At the Christmas Stroll?"

Noel hadn't meant to bring her problems to work, but it appeared that they'd gotten the better of her. Why couldn't she have been a better actor? She exhaled a sigh as she met Tate's eyes. "No, Tate. I'm sorry. I actually had a great time with you."

"Me too," Tate said, still giving her a deep look, like he was trying to read her soul.

"It's just—" Noel stopped herself, shaking her head. "No, sorry."

"Noel, hey, what is it?" Tate pressed.

Noel felt her lips part to speak, but she hesitated before a single word came out. What was she doing? What was going on between them? What was she supposed to do? She frowned, then exhaled another sigh. "Last night my ex-husband showed up at the door."

Tate's smile dropped even further. "Oh."

"Yeah, he apologized for what he did and asked me and the kids to move back in with him."

Tate looked away. "I see. Isn't that good news then?"

"I'm not sure. I mean maybe. The truth is that my apartment search and promise to be out by the twenty-fourth isn't exactly going as planned. Don't get me wrong; this job has been great, but I barely have enough for a deposit and first month's rent. Most places want first and last month, and most places aren't available until after the holidays." Noel sighed again. "Plus, I haven't been able to think about Christmas shopping for the kids. It's all just moving really fast, and if I move back with Bryan, I don't have to worry about any of that."

Tate gave a shallow nod. "I see."

They both stared at the oven for a long moment afterward, neither knowing what to say. Noel supposed that part of her wanted to hear what Tate would say. How he'd react. Would he try to get her to stay like one of those stereotypical romance novels she'd read? Who was she kidding? They'd just met and weren't even dating. She wasn't even sure if he actually liked her. Plus, what about her vow to quit men for the time being?

Tate's gaze shifted toward the counter.

Noel followed it, looking to see what he was staring at, when she noticed a Christmas Cup filled with donations.

"Ever since I went by and saw the light display at your dad's house, I've been thinking about *It's a Wonderful Life*," Tate said.

Noel looked at him as he continued staring at the cup. "Oh, yeah? You saw the display? Well, it's a great movie. It was my mother's favorite."

"Yeah, not for the judging just yet. I went on my own. And interesting. Mine too." He paused and looked up to meet her eyes again. "It got me thinking about how George wondered what the world and community would be like without him in it. How the choices we make affect others, even in ways we don't realize."

"Very astute of you," Noel said. "What made you think that?"

Tate waited a long moment before replying. "You."

"Me?" Noel couldn't hide the surprise in her voice.

Tate nodded. "Yeah. You. If I hadn't decided to move to Glenn Hills, I never would have met you. When my wife died, it was easy to wonder what life would have been like had I not been there. Would Alice have lived? I don't know, but as hard as it was, I made the choice to continue on. I moved away, I opened the coffee shop, then I met you. What would have happened if I didn't open the coffee shop? Would someone else have taken a chance on hiring you? Would you have met another man? Would you have moved back in with your ex? Look, I'm not saying that you shouldn't move back in with him. All I'm saying is that our lives collided for whatever reason. Maybe I'm only supposed to be in your life for a short bit to help you realize whatever it is you need to realize, just like Clarence the angel was for George. And maybe you're in my life for a short bit, to help me realize whatever it is that I need to realize. Either way, I can't help but think that our lives intersected for a reason."

Noel tried to make sense of everything Tate was telling her. He was saying that the decisions they'd both made had led them to this point in their lives, which was true. But did he feel that way because he felt he might want to be with her, or was it because he was supposed to help her realize what she needed to do next? So many questions and so much uncertainty. First Tom's story about almost giving up on the life he had with Holly, which eventually had led to Noel being born. Now Tate telling her he felt that life had led them to this point together for a reason? But what was the reason? And what would she give up if she chose either path?

"Are you saying you feel a connection between us?" Noel looked up at him. Her heart raced as her words fell between them. What if he told her he didn't feel the same? She'd embarrass herself in her place of work. Is that what she was supposed to do in order to realize the path to follow was the one with Bryan?

"I'm saying that you've made an impact on my life, and that coming to Glenn Hills feels like the right thing to have done in this moment. As for a connection, I don't want to cloud your judgment. Moving on from Alice has been near impossible. It's taken a year and a half to get here, and I'm still not sure if I'll ever be ready to date again. Maybe eventually I will, and maybe eventually it'd be you I'd date. Who knows if we'd work out, or if you'd even like me? What I'm saying is yes, there's a possibility of something between us. But right now, that's all it is. A possibility. I don't want it to come down to a decision between me and your ex. Your decision should come down to what you feel is right, and which life path you feel you can't go on without knowing."

Tate set a hand on Noel's shoulder, and she gazed over at him. As much as she hadn't wanted to hear it, she knew he was right. There wasn't a clear path for her to follow. If she stayed, maybe she'd find an apartment, maybe the kids would like their schools, maybe she'd continue her job, and maybe she and Tate would end up together. But if she went, maybe the kids would like their old schools better, maybe they'd be financially secure, and maybe she and Bryan could find a way to be happy. All maybes. No certainty. The only way she'd figure it out was by choosing a path, and for whatever reason, her choices, and the choices of everyone in her life, had led her to where she was now.

The bell chimed as someone walked through the door.

Tate released her shoulder, and suddenly Noel felt her hand reach for his. Their fingers touched for just a second, and their eyes locked on each other. Butterflies swirled about in her stomach as her mind spun with possibilities. But a second later, it was gone. Their hands dropped as a woman and her daughter made their way to the counter.

"I better get to work on some of the bills," Tate said. "But let me know if you want to talk some more later."

Noel nodded, letting his words run through her head again as she watched him disappear from sight. She turned to the customers and smiled. "Sorry about that. What can I get you?"

That night, Noel lay in bed with Brittany on one side and Evan on the other. All three tossed and turned.

"Do you think we actually might win the Christmas Cup Competition tomorrow?" they kept asking.

Noel heard the floorboards creaking in the other room, most likely Tom pacing anxiously as well. On several occasions she heard Trevor open and close the living room door, which likely meant he was up, peeking outside to see if anyone was outside watching their Christmas display.

There was no denying it—as incredible as the Garcetti house had been, they each still hung onto a shred of hope that maybe the crowds they'd been drawing meant they might actually be able to win. It would be a Christmas present the kids would never forget, but Noel had to keep reminding them that even if they didn't win, it was the experience that mattered. The real reason Noel couldn't sleep wasn't because of her kids tossing and turning, however, or even because of the Christmas Cup Competition winner's announcement the next day. It was the decision she had in front of her. The decision that would affect her and her family's future, forever. Which path to take.

In the other room, she heard a quiet but audible shuffling of feet. She knew it was Trevor, probably checking on the crowd. She took a deep breath, thinking of how much she longed for him to win. Just like her, Trevor had closed himself off, and a big reason for that was because of her. She knew that she hadn't been there in the ways he needed and that most of her attention had gone to his younger brother and sister. He'd always put on such a brave face, and most of the time she didn't know what she could even say. He was getting older so fast now. But she wanted to be there. She was his mother, and he needed her.

She slipped out of bed while trying not to disrupt Evan and Brittany from their slumbers. When she reached the end of the hall, she noticed Trevor in his pajamas, curled into a ball by the window in the living room. He was looking out at a car that had slowed to look at the house.

"Were there a lot of cars tonight?" she asked softly. Trevor's head snapped toward her, startled. He jumped up, realizing he'd been caught.

"Uh. I was just checking if any lights had gone out. I was about to go back to bed," he sputtered.

Noel laughed. "It's okay, Trevor. You can sit back down. I'll sit with you."

Trevor waited a moment, obviously unsure of whether this was some sort of joke. Noel took a seat on the ground at the window across from where he'd been sitting, and a second later, Trevor sat back down.

They each looked out the window. Another car slowed to observe the house.

"You guys really did a good job on the house," she started.

"It was mostly Grandpa. But yeah, people seem to like it."

She felt herself smile at his modesty. "I think you had a big part in it too. I'm glad to see you spending so much time with your grandpa too. I can tell that he's really enjoyed it."

"Really?" Trevor asked in surprise.

"Yeah, he's been a lot happier lately. Your grandpa isn't an easy man to deal with, but he means well, and he really cares about you. It's made me very happy to see you two together like this."

"Well, I've enjoyed spending time with him too. He and Richard are funny. And I've learned a lot about electricity."

Noel laughed, picturing the boring lessons on electricity that she herself had sat through on hundreds of occasions over the years. Just then, one of the cars turned its headlights on and pulled away.

Noel looked over to Trevor, observing the wonder in his face as he looked out the window to the magnificent display and onlookers taking it in just outside.

"You know, I've never really talked to you much about things since your dad passed, and I'm sorry for that." She took a deep breath, and Trevor looked over at her. She continued. "You've put up with a lot, and you've been so strong through everything. When I brought Bryan into your life, you never once complained even though I could tell you didn't care for him." She tried to fight off tears that she felt surfacing.

"I knew that Bryan made you happy. And I didn't want to bother you. I knew how hard it was for you and I didn't want to be one more thing you had to worry about. It hurt me seeing how sad you always were." Trevor looked down, fidgeting with his fingers.

His words felt like a dagger in her heart. "I'm so sorry, Trevor." She felt at a loss for words, and this time she couldn't hold back. Tears began to form in her eyes.

"Don't cry, Mom." She looked up and laughed, wiping her eyes with her pajama sleeve.

"Sorry. I'm just really proud of you. And I want you to know how much I love you."

Trevor looked down, and Noel could see that he, too, was trying to suppress tears. He looked up, and she watched as a tear streamed down his cheek. He stayed quiet for a long while, and she decided not to push him.

"I miss Dad," he finally said before breaking into sobs.

Noel's heart sank. She watched as Trevor began to break down, and in that moment she stood and walked over to him. He looked up, and Noel sat beside him and put her arm around his back and pulled him into her lap. He fell over and began to cry harder. Noel felt herself cry as well. Her body full of pent-up emotion, a longing to be there for her son who needed her so badly.

"Me too," Noel returned through her tears. "Me too."

Trevor continued to cry in her lap, his body convulsing from the sobs as she cried with him, holding him in one arm and rubbing his back with her other hand. She wanted so badly to do more for him. To give him all the gifts she knew he wanted for Christmas. To give him his father back. To let him win the Christmas Cup Competition. But she knew that none of that was possible, and that in this moment, all he really needed was simply her.

After another couple minutes of crying, Trevor's sob began to grow softer. A moment later, he sat back up, and Noel wiped away her tears as well.

"I just want you to be happy, Mom," he said, his eyes red and puffy. "You deserve it. I hope you know that."

Noel let out a long, labored breath. She was the one who was supposed to be doing the comforting, and yet here was Trevor saying things to her that comforted her in ways he'd probably never know. Reassurance that he cared and also that he knew how much she cared for him.

"You know, you're pretty great. I'm lucky to have a son like you."

He smiled and she rubbed her hands in his hair.

"I want you to know that if you ever need to talk, I'm here. And in all the decisions I make, I'm always thinking about you first. I want to know what you think. Do you like your new school?" Noel asked.

"It's not bad actually. And I know, Mom. I know," he replied. They both laughed some more, and the last car parked outside turned on its lights. They both continued to sit there together in silence, each just taking in the moment as it was. A mother and her son.

Trevor wiped his face again with his sleeve, and Noel took another deep breath before slowly getting to her feet. "Okay, let's get some sleep. That's enough tears for one night."

Trevor stood too. "Okay."

They walked together out of the living room, and Trevor turned to head back into the family room.

"Trevor," she said, stopping him. He turned. "Whatever happens, I want you to know that what you've done in decorating the house is very special, and it's made my Christmas magical. Now try to get some sleep."

Trevor tried to hide a grin. "Thanks, Mom. I love you."

"I love you, Trevor."

Trevor turned to head into the family room, and Noel watched as he disappeared around the corner. A moment later, she slipped back into her bedroom, a large weight lifted and a feeling of peace resonating inside her.

CHAPTER 22

TUESDAY, DECEMBER 22

Tom had been off-kilter the entire day, knots churning in his stomach. The first thing was the absence of his usual Tuesday morning breakfast with Richard at Bertha's Diner. He'd thought about going alone, but something about that just didn't feel right. He still hadn't been back to see Richard after Richard had insisted Tom come forward with the truth. It wasn't Richard's decision or place. He, of all people, knew that Tom wasn't the type of man to be told what to do. The old sap needed to mind his own business. Tom didn't want to think about what would happen if Richard were to take a turn for the worse, but still, just because Richard was in bad health didn't mean he was right.

The other reason for his nerves was, the night before, a big bus full of people had come by their house for a long while to inspect and judge it for the Christmas Cup Competition. Along with the thirty or so judges, there had been at least three hundred people checking out the display. He supposed the large crowd didn't hurt his chances, but still, could they actually win?

Tom had noticed Tate in the mix, chatting it up with several of the other judges. Might he have an impact in helping them to win? Surely he knew Noel's situation and felt for her and the kids. Noel and Tate had even been walking together at the Christmas Stroll, and Tom wasn't a stranger to the looks he'd seen them exchange with each other. He could tell that there was definitely some sort of spark between them. In Tom's mind, that was a heck of a lot better than sparks between Noel and Bryan. That weasel had a lot of nerve coming back into his daughter and grandkids' lives like that. Tom still wished he could have given him a piece of his mind, but that was that and the moment was gone.

Night had fallen, and the biggest storm California had seen in years was beginning to show itself. Strong gusts of wind and several inches of hard falling rain, mixed with the chilly winter air, meant the Glenn Hills Christmas Cup Competition winner's ceremony would be held indoors at the town hall.

Tom followed Noel and the kids as they made their way toward the front of the crowd. The auditorium was loud, with hundreds of people crammed together to make their way inside. Ahead, on the stage, were the judges, all sitting behind the podium with the large gold Cup shining atop it. He noticed the Garcetti family glad-handing with families around them. The wife stood with four other women, laughing loudly. Kayla, the daughter, glanced in their direction and smiled when she noticed Trevor.

Trevor gave her a shy wave and blushed hard before turning back to the front.

Tom looked over to Alex, who gave him a wink. *Nothing like a schmoozer*, Tom thought. He hadn't set out on this journey to lose, of course, but when the Garcettis had shown up at Tom's house and stolen the attention of the crowd to announce their own lighting ceremony, Tom had never wanted to win more in his life. Seeing the devastated look on Trevor's face when they saw the Garcettis' Christmas light display had been like a dagger in the heart. But the town hadn't stopped talking about the possibility of a VanHansen comeback. Everyone loved a story of an underdog, didn't they?

The crowd quieted as a tall lanky man in a red suit and green tie stood and walked toward the podium. Tom recognized him as the annoying mayor he saw in the *Glenn Hills Times* all too often lately. He gave the crowd a goofy smile and tapped on the microphone, sending feedback thundering through the room. "Whoops!" He laughed hard. "Sorry about that folks." He flashed a toothy grin.

The crowd quieted some more. Slowly, all attention focused on the man. Noel grabbed onto Brittany's hand in front of them, and Trevor put his arm around Evan.

"Welcome to the Annual Glenn Hills Christmas Cup Competition!"

The crowd burst into cheers and applause. Tom's hands went flying to his ears. Couldn't the crowd keep it down a bit? His breathing quickened as his heart began to thump harder.

"All right, all right," the man said, waving them off with another laugh. "I'm Mayor Hawthorn, and I couldn't be happier to be standing here tonight to announce this year's winner."

Again, the crowd burst into cheers. Someone whistled loud from the back. The lanky, goofy mayor continued to laugh until the cheers died down.

Tom glanced over to the judges sitting behind him and noticed Tate smiling at Noel. Noel glanced in Tate's direction for a moment before turning back to the mayor. Smiling was always a good sign. Did that mean Tate knew there was good news coming?

"All right, let's get to the good stuff," the mayor continued. "This year, we have broken the record for most donations of all time for the Christmas Cup Competition, totaling $16,812."

People gasped and then cheered at the amount. Trevor turned back to meet Tom's eyes, full of hope. Tom looked over to the Garcetti family, each clapping while smiling wide, also full of hope. Sixteen thousand dollars was a heck of a lot of money, and if anyone could use it about now, it was Noel, and the kids.

The crowd quieted. "Without further ado, let's announce the winner." Tom's heart beat harder and harder against the anticipation and nervous tension in the building, making him feel like a kid again, filled with excitement. A moment later, the mayor looked up from an envelope and smiled big for all to see. Tom held his breath as he waited for the words to come. "The winner of $16,812 and the Christmas Cup Competition is . . ." The mayor waited another second, letting the anticipation build some more. "The Garcetti family!"

The crowd burst into cheers and applause.

As though in slow motion, Tom saw Trevor gaze back at him, tears welling up in his eyes. Brittany and Evan frowned, their faces full of defeat. Noel's expression dropped as she moved in to hug her kids. Tom glanced over at the Garcettis, the crowd around them chanting and cheering as each of them hugged the people around them, smiling wide for all to see. Samantha looked over at Noel, and for a second, her expression shifted into something more somber. But then another woman came up to hug her and Samantha's attention was pulled back to the celebration. Finally, the realization settled in for Tom. His heart sank like a brick in the ocean. His head was spinning as the noise pulsed around them. A wave of sadness overtook him, leaving him with an empty feeling of despair.

He'd put himself out there and had been defeated again. Only this time, the stakes had been much higher. They'd needed that money. So much for the underdog story.

The kids were devastated, Noel was devastated, and Tom was devastated for all of them.

Alex led the charge up the stairs as his wife and kids followed behind, each smiling big as the crowd continued to cheer them on.

Tom noticed Tate's mournful look from the stage, and some of the other judges who also seemed to share his sentiments. For a second, he even thought he heard boos from the crowd. His heart continued to race from the chaos as Alex made his way to the podium. All Tom could think, as the room grew fuzzier, was that he'd let his family down. His breath felt impossible to catch. The cheers became one ear-piercing, high-pitch buzz. Tom's chest felt as though it were tightening around him. Then something stabbed at the back of his skull, like a knife was ripping through it from the inside.

"Tom?" Noel said.

Tom's eyes went in and out of focus as he tried to find her through the pain in his head and side.

"Tom?" she said again. "Dad!"

He heard the cheers fade as people around them began to scream and rush toward him. His heart rate spiked some more. Air escaped his grasp completely as his chest constricted tighter. He felt a hand on his shoulder and heard people around him, but the buzzing grew louder and his vision blurred until it turned to a bright white. His hand shot out to catch onto something, anything, for balance, but he couldn't feel anything. He couldn't breathe.

With one more rock backward, his body fell off balance. He slammed into the ground. Everything went still.

CHAPTER 23

WEDNESDAY, DECEMBER 23

His eyes opened slowly to a steady chirping gnawing at his ears. Everything felt bright and cloudy, like he was floating in the sky. He rubbed at his eyes until his vision cleared a bit, and soon, Tom realized he was in a strange bed in some sort of white room.

"Well say it ain't so," a familiar raspy voice croaked from his side.

Tom turned his head slowly until his eyes reached a figure. His vision was still blurry, and at his side, the bright light was even brighter. He rubbed his eyes some more, until he realized that the bright light was actually the window, and the figure was Richard.

"Where am I?" Tom groaned.

"They didn't tell you?" Richard smiled a weak, toothy smile, waiting for Tom to react. "You're in hell. It's just you and me in this tiny room for the rest of time."

Tom shot up, or at least tried to, but then realized he couldn't move more than a couple of inches. His chest felt heavy, and his arm was strapped into something. He looked over to see an IV tube sticking out of his arm. A blue gown covered his body, and blue socks covered his feet. On the other side of the room, Richard had the same setup. The same blue gown, the same IV, and the same socks on an uncomfortable plastic bed. Was this a dream? A nightmare? The chirping began to speed up faster, like a police scanner approaching its target.

"Okay. Okay. Calm down," Richard said. "It's a joke. You're in the hospital. You had a heart attack."

Tom turned toward him. "What? What are you talking about?" He tried comprehending what was happening, rewinding to his last clear memory, but everything felt fuzzy. His chest hurt. His head throbbed. His arms felt weak, and his back sore. This was from a heart attack? How was that possible?

Suddenly, it came to him: The Christmas Cup Competition ceremony. The look on Trevor's face when they found out they'd lost. The Garcetti family shaking hands and hugging people around them as the crowd cheered them on. The $16,000 prize. The pain he felt because of it.

"Hate to say it, but I told you so," Richard rasped.

"Told me what?" Tom asked.

"Told you this would happen. Your eating habits. Your diabetes and heart disease. Skipping your doctor's visits."

Tom felt himself flush with anger. The heart monitor's chirping became faster as he felt his blood pressure rise. "What happened? Am I going to be okay? Why are my back and head in so much pain?"

"Slow down, Turbo. You had a heart attack and then you fell. Bumped your head pretty hard, I guess. The doctor said it was major. You're lucky to be here. Your daughter and grandkids were here all night." He paused a moment, gathering himself. "I told her."

Tom darted a look toward Richard that felt like it was filled with daggers. "Told her what?" He heard voices approaching from outside the doorway. The voices grew louder, and a second later, he recognized them.

"Is he going to live?" Trevor asked.

Noel darted through the doorway, with three kids at her sides. Four sets of eyes stared in from the edge of the room, then fixed on Tom.

Tom swallowed the dry lump in his throat.

"I'm sorry ma'am, but he should really only have one visitor at a time," a woman's voice said from behind the group.

"Trevor, can you watch Brittany and Evan in the waiting room for a moment?" Noel said. "I'll be there soon."

Trevor hesitated for a second before grabbing Evan and Brittany's hands and then walking off.

Noel shot in to his side like a missile, her face flushed with fury. "Heart disease? Diabetes? You didn't think it was important to tell me?" she shouted. Her eyes were red and puffy and her eyebrows furrowed.

"All right, no more lies. What happened that night with the accident? With Mom?"

Tom stared and then glanced to Richard.

"Nope. He's not getting you out of this," Noel snapped. "Tom, you better tell me the truth this instant."

Tom's head swirled. It was back to Tom now? Richard had done this? Given him up? He felt like leaping up from his bed to lash out. Another part of him just wanted to make it right. She knew, and there was no more hiding it.

"Yes, I have heart disease and diabetes," Tom confessed. "I didn't know you guys would be coming home, and I didn't think it was relevant if you were only staying for a little while."

Noel was trembling. "Relevant? Relevant? You didn't think it was relevant to let your daughter know that you had some major health issues that could give you a heart attack at a moment's notice? Like say at the Christmas Cup Competition announcement? What if it had been while you were driving?"

Her words shot through his heart, and he felt his cheeks go warm. The chirps from the monitor sped up. Tom took a deep breath and let his calm come back to him before finally opening his mouth to speak.

"The night Holly died," The words choked in his mouth, as tears began to well up in his eyes, "I had a heart attack. My foot went numb and heavy. I hit the accelerator, and we sped straight into the median. It was my fault." He felt his tears begin to pour out in the face of the memory he'd pushed away for so long. The pain he'd felt in his chest and legs. The fear in Holly's eyes. Her hands scrambling for the steering wheel as she screamed, asking him what was wrong. Her lifeless body beside him, head slumped forward, glass shards in her hair. The ambulance carrying her away and prying him out of the car. Then her still, beautiful face as she lay on the hospital bed, alone.

Tom looked up to see Noel wiping away tears of her own and shaking her head.

"So what? You thought if you didn't tell me what happened and if you pushed me and your grandkids away, we'd just forget about you? Let you live alone until you had another heart attack and died? Is that it?" Her voice was loud, hostile.

Tom cringed, trying to stop the tears. "I thought if I pushed you away, then you wouldn't have to feel the pain of another parent dying.

You'd grow distant and maybe even grow to hate me. I thought it would make it easier for you when my time came too. And I'd deserve it because I was the one who killed her."

Noel stared at him for a long, hard moment, clearly incredulous. She seemed to be considering his words, possibly realizing that maybe he'd had a point. "You idiot." Her words were slow and deliberate. "You really haven't figured it out, have you?"

Tom tilted his head in confusion.

"I didn't want to be more distant. I didn't want to hate you so that it'd be easier. The only thing I wish I had with Mom is more time."

As she said the words, Tom understood completely. If he and Holly had been on bad terms, he knew it wouldn't have made anything easier. In fact, he'd probably only have more regrets for not being closer. But in the days, months, and years after her death, all he'd been able to think about was that he didn't deserve life anymore, and that he'd do anything to make sure his family never felt the way he did about Holly when they lost him too.

"Did you ever stop to think that maybe instead of pushing me away, you could have been there to help comfort me? And that maybe I could have been there to help comfort you?" Noel continued.

"I didn't think I deserved comfort. I could have eaten better or exercised more to prevent it. I'm the reason she died. Me!"

"Listen to me, Tom! You didn't choose to have a heart attack while driving. It was beyond your control. But I'm your daughter, and I deserved to know what happened. I also deserve the right to choose for myself whether I'm in your life or not. I want a father for as long as I can have one, and the kids want a grandfather for as long as they can have one. So please, please, stop pushing us away. Let us in. Even if it's only for an hour, or for twenty more years, let us in." Tears began to trickle down her cheeks.

Tom stared for what felt like minutes, but what was really probably only seconds. He finally understood what Richard had been trying to tell him for so long. Noel was right; she and the kids deserved a father and grandfather figure in their lives. They deserved more time with him, and he needed to be the man that they needed, not the man he'd chosen to become.

"Okay," was all he said.

Noel smiled weakly through the tears. "That also means getting back to treatment."

Tom let out a deep breath. "Yeah, we'll see about that."

Noel's eyes narrowed. "What are you talking about? Did you not just tell me 'okay' to being the father and grandfather we deserve?"

"Sorry," Tom said. "I meant that I don't know if I can do treatment, because I don't know if I can afford it. The government only pays for so much, and the rest comes out of my monthly allowance. After Holly's death, my savings dried up fast. And then when you guys moved back in . . . well, just don't worry about it."

"No, tell me."

Tom sighed. "The bills are adding up. I'm in the negative."

Noel's breathing quickened, her mind clearly churning. "Well that's my problem. If you need help, why didn't you just ask me? Look. You need to get some rest, but stop worrying about the money. I'm going to find a way to get a home. I'm going to find a way to put food on the table. I'm going to find a way to get Christmas presents for the kids. And I'm going to find a way to make sure you can stay afloat."

Tom lifted his hand to combat her points.

Noel mirrored the gesture right back at him. "Just get some rest. I need you. The kids need you."

Tom didn't respond.

Noel turned back toward the door but hesitated before walking forward, looking over her shoulder. "I love you, Dad."

Her words hung in the air for a long while after she disappeared out of sight. Tom tried to make sense of everything that had happened. She'd said that she loved him and had called him Dad, but he hadn't replied. What if that was the last time she'd see him? What if he had another heart attack and died? She'd go on without ever hearing him tell her one last time that he loved her too.

"Well, this is awkward," a voice rasped from across the room.

Tom glanced over at Richard, smirking from the bed on the other side. He'd almost completely forgotten about him being there, watching the whole thing go down. Tom didn't know how to feel. On one hand, it hadn't been Richard's place to butt in and tell Noel like that. Tom had warned him to stay out of it. On the other hand, Tom knew he'd been wrong. Noel was right: pushing them away hadn't been the right thing to do. They had a right to know what had happened, and they also had a right to know about his heart disease and heart attack. On top of it all, he'd missed his friend the past week. Sticking to his guns and pushing Richard away had been just as hard as pushing away his family.

"Of all the places they could put me, it had to be next to you?" Tom finally said.

Richard smiled. "There's the Tom I know. I'm sure they figured pairing together two old geezers at the end of their days would go off without a hitch. We could gripe about being old together."

Tom shrugged. "You know how they say you're as old as you feel?"

Richard nodded.

"Well I feel older than I ever have before, and I don't much care for it."

"You know, back when I was a kid, I never considered that I'd be anything other than as young as I was then. I thought I'd stay that way forever. Always carefree, pain-free, jubilant. Boy, do I miss those days."

Tom knew exactly how he felt because he, too, had felt like that. For years he went through life thinking he was never going to age. That things would be okay year after year after year. But slowly and surely, life had crept in to wake him up to the fact that he wasn't that young kid anymore.

"We're just two old geezers, going through this little thing called life together," Richard said.

A nurse came in to take their vitals. She asked if she could get them anything and then left them alone together, yet again.

Tom gazed over to Richard, taking in his aged, fragile-looking friend with wispy hair and a pale, wrinkled face. "Hey, Putz."

Richard looked over. "Yeah, Turbo?"

"Thanks."

Richard simply nodded.

To some, that may have seemed to be just a simple, vague offering, but to Tom and Richard, the thanks was an acknowledgment of a gratitude far deeper than the definition of the word itself.

CHAPTER 24

THURSDAY, DECEMBER 24

Noel rested her arms against the counter. Finally, the afternoon rush had begun to fade. "Jingle Bells" hummed in the background as the heater pumped out hot air to warm them against the cold weather just outside. Raindrops continued to beat against the window in a steady pattern. No sleep had come to her the night before, and she'd been going through the motions all day—tired and consumed by her thoughts as more and more holiday shoppers had come by for coffees, cocoas, and holiday treats.

Not that her life had ever been simple, but why couldn't anything be easier? Why couldn't she and the kids simply be enjoying the Christmas season, wrapping presents, all while Tom watched his old western movies from the recliner, with Richard home with Christie? She knew the answer, and that was because lately life hadn't been going her way. As much as she'd wanted it to, she always knew that another curveball would be right around the corner.

The gray swirling clouds moved about as another hard gust of rain slammed against the window. Then the door swung open and with it came a strong, cool breeze.

"Look who's back," Tate said cheerily, closing his umbrella and shaking off the rain. He was wearing a red sweater accompanied by a red Santa cap. "I thought you'd still be at the hospital. How's Tom doing?"

Noel didn't answer. She walked to the sink to wash her hands while Tate made his way around the counter.

"I'm sorry. Did I say something wrong? Sorry if it was busy. I've been running errands around town."

Noel dried her hands, then looked up to meet Tate's eyes. She let out a deep breath. "No, sorry. Just a lot going on."

"Want to tell me about it? Is Tom okay?"

Noel stared into Tate's eyes. "He's okay for now. It was a heart attack. Turns out it wasn't his first. He's had heart disease for years, and he'd had another heart attack the night he crashed into a median and my mom died."

Tate set a hand on her shoulder. "Oh, Noel."

Noel nodded. "It's fine. Just don't want to deal with another death. Haven't I already suffered enough? First my husband, then my mom, now my dad? Well I hope not, but you know what I mean." Her gaze fell to the floor.

"That's what I used to think too, except I blamed myself for what happened to Alice," Tate said. "Actually, I still do."

Noel considered asking him about it but again reminded herself that when he was ready, he would talk about it himself.

Tate looked down to the gold wedding band on his finger. "It was up in Oregon," he said.

Noel glanced up with curiosity.

"That's where I was born and raised. She was too. We were high school sweethearts. I was the basketball team captain, and she was the head cheerleader. As cliché as it gets. After college, I worked as a marketing executive at a big firm and she was a coffee buyer for Dean's Coffee, an up-and-coming coffee chain. She was always in South America looking for the best and most unique blends. She convinced me to come along on one of her trips to Colombia. I figured while we were down there, we might as well have some fun, so we went zip-lining." Tate drew in a long and deep breath before he continued, clearly starting to get choked up.

He continued. "I took off down the zip line first. When I looked back to see her coming, I waited a good ten minutes. The worker at the bottom insisted she must have gotten scared and that she'd be down soon enough, but she never came."

For a second, it looked like Tate was about to burst into tears, but he held them back. "Turns out her harness hadn't been fastened properly. She fell over a hundred feet and landed on her back. Medic said she died instantly."

"Oh, Tate." Noel put her hand on his arm for comfort as he looked down. All signs of his light-hearted and confident manly-man demeanor were gone.

"Her parents blamed me. Truthfully, I do too. I started drinking, quit my job, kept to myself. Finally, one morning after sitting down at the bar down the street from me, I just sat there without ordering a drink. I don't know what happened, but all of a sudden I had this overwhelming feeling of peace and clarity. That's when I looked for the spot a thousand miles away. I stopped drinking, and the next day I packed my stuff and headed for California. Opened the coffee shop to remember her with every passing day." Tate looked up to meet her eyes, then laughed out of embarrassment. "Sorry. Didn't mean to get all sentimental. Just felt like it was time you knew. Whether you decide to move back with your ex or not."

She touched his hand. "I'm sure you don't need to hear it from another person, but it's not your fault. The one thing I've learned through my losses is that when it's time, it's time. And things seem to happen for a reason, always leading us down the next path."

Tate nodded slowly, giving her a half-smile.

Noel thought again about what Tate had said the other day when she'd told him about Bryan coming back. About how maybe there was something between them, and maybe eventually they'd even go on a date, but that there couldn't be any promises. It was all maybes and pos-sibilities. Nothing was certain. Even if she stayed, maybe they wouldn't work out. Her relationship with Tate was such a question mark. She was only just beginning to realize that she barely knew him. "I guess there really is a lot we don't know about each other, isn't there?"

Tate nodded, smiling back at her. "We're only at the beginning of what could be a very long or very short road."

Noel stared at him. The bearded, rugged man in the Santa cap. The man who loved to smile and joke whenever he got the chance. The man who loved a good cup of coffee and knew how to brew one. The man who'd taken a chance on her when no one else would. The man who'd opened up about his past and his wife, and who'd shared laughs both at the shop and at the Christmas Stroll. The man who'd taken an interest in her kids and her father. This was a very good man.

Then she thought of Bryan and the road they'd already started. How much easier it would be to go back to the world she and the kids knew. To give him another chance because he, too, had good in him. The handsome, clean-cut man who looked so much like Jacob that sometimes she forgot it wasn't him. Where else could she find a man so good looking, so caring, and so familiar? It was time she finally went to the inn to see him.

She knew what she had to do for herself and her kids.

Tom and Richard lay on their beds as the rain continued to beat against the window just outside. The doctor came in to check their vitals and let them know they'd each need to stay in through Christmas, just as a precaution. Richard's tests showed possible brain trauma, even though he felt just fine, and even better as the days had gone by. The doctor wanted him to stay so that they could watch to ensure the blood flow was moving correctly to his brain.

Tom was to stay because his heart disease had spiked his blood pressure through the roof. The doctor hadn't been shy about mentioning that heart disease was arguably the number one killer in America, and that it was also known as the silent assassin because you rarely saw it coming.

"I'm really just keeping you both here so that you can be miserable together. Merry Christmas," the doctor said before letting out a chuckle and then leaving them to themselves.

A moment later, footsteps approached, and the kids shot inside.

"Grandpa!" Evan screamed. He ran to the bedside while Brittany and Trevor followed behind. Noel poked her head in but then picked up a phone call and disappeared back out of the room.

"Hello there, Evan," Tom croaked. He smoothed out his blue gown to make sure it didn't ride up too high on his pale, weak legs.

"Are you and Richard going to die?"

Tom felt his eyes go wide.

"Evan!" Trevor snapped.

Richard laughed from across the room as Tom scrambled for a response.

"I hope not. But eventually everyone does." Tom wasn't one to sugarcoat things.

"But when we do eventually die, hopefully we'll be up in heaven with your dad and grandmother. And we'll get to see you again too someday," Richard added.

"Promise?" Evan asked.

"Promise."

Evan smiled and so did Brittany and Trevor.

Oh, the religion talk. Tom hadn't ever been too outspoken on his religious beliefs, but through his years, he'd always believed in God and in the plan he had for everyone, including Tom himself. He liked to think there was a heaven, and he knew that if there was, Holly was up there waiting for him. Now it was a matter of if he was worthy to make it to her. But boy did he miss her, and boy did he hope so.

"What are you hoping Santa brings for Christmas?" Richard asked.

All three kids turned toward him, grinning from ear to ear. Definitely a question they wanted to be asked.

"A dog!" Evan promptly shouted.

"Yeah, a dog!" Brittany added.

"Oh a dog, huh?" Richard said. "You know dogs are a lot to take care of. Have you been enjoying your time with Christie?"

Brittany and Evan nodded shyly.

"Well, she's been enjoying her time with you too. But your grandpa was telling me you might want a basketball, Evan. And Brittany, you might want ballet slippers. Is that true?"

They both nodded again, each hardly able to contain their smiles.

Richard turned to Trevor. "And what about you, Trevor? What are you hoping to get for Christmas?"

Trevor hesitated, glancing at Tom briefly before bursting into an answer. "A Playstation. I've never had one, and all the kids at school are talking about it."

"Is Kayla one of those kids?" Tom asked.

Trevor's face went red. "Yeah. Maybe."

Tom nodded. He stared at the spiky-haired boy dressed in a brown sweater and jeans. He almost looked like a different boy altogether. His rough exterior had been nothing but a facade, hiding the boy he'd tried to lock away through all the years of moving from place to place, school after school, doing his best to watch over his brother, sister, and mother.

"Well, remember, Christmas isn't about the presents; it's about being with the ones you love, and appreciating what you already have," Richard said.

All three kids nodded their agreement, even though Tom knew they probably didn't see it that way yet.

An unexpected pain shot up Tom's leg, through his bones, and suddenly his heartbeat began to spike.

Richard turned to see it. "Kids, why don't you head back over to the waiting area. Tom and I need to take a little rest."

Tom bit his lip in agony as the pain continued to surge through his thigh.

"Okay. Bye, Grandpa. Bye, Richard," Brittany said.

"Bye, kids," Richard returned.

"We'll see you soon," Tom added through the pain, watching as each of his grandkids turned slowly and walked back through the door.

"I pressed the button for the nurse," Richard said as soon as they were gone.

But just like that, the pain was gone. "I'm fine now. Just a little neuropathy or something."

Richard shook his head. "I hate being old."

Tom nodded.

"You know, you've got to get better," Richard said. "You've got to push through this thing. Go back to treatment. Those kids love you so much, and they need you right now. You've got to push through, for them."

Tom turned back to Richard. "I'm trying, Richard. But if there's one thing I've learned, it's that we have no control over when our time is coming, and right now, I can feel it just around the corner."

"Well, let's keep fighting it together."

CHAPTER 25

FRIDAY, DECEMBER 25

Tom opened his eyes on Christmas morning to the sound of a steady chirp from the IV, and a constant rain beating against the window outside. He let out a giant yawn and stretched under the itchy blue hospital gown. "Well, never thought I'd be saying this, but Merry Christmas, Richard," Tom said with a laugh as he blinked the sleep out of his eyes.

Who would have thought he'd be spending Christmas in the hospital with Richard at his side?

Thinking about it, so much had changed in such a short amount of time, turning his life upside down almost completely. Noel being back, the kids, the Christmas Cup Competition, almost winning it, Richard's stroke, the heart attack, and even Noel's forgiveness. Who would have thought that grumpy old Tom would be reunited with his family once again, just in time for Christmas? The anniversary of his and Holly's marriage.

"Did I send you into shock by wishing you a Merry Christmas?" Tom quipped. He let out a chuckle, waiting for Richard's reaction. "Richard?"

He looked over to Richard, but the bed was empty. *Odd*, Tom thought. He sat up and the beat of his heart monitor began to quicken. Where was he? He looked up, confused, when a nurse rushed through the doorway.

She glanced from him to the empty bed, and then she understood.

"I'm sorry, Mr. VanHansen. Mr. Sampson had a blood clot. You stayed asleep under the pills you were on when we came in last night." She paused, but her story wasn't making any sense. Where was Richard now then? "I'm sorry to be the one to tell you this, but Mr. Sampson passed away."

The words felt like a dream at first, but when they sank in, they punched him head on. His stomach dropped. He felt hollow inside. And then his eyes welled up.

The nurse set a hand on Tom's shoulder, but his body had gone so numb he couldn't even feel it. Her words passed in one ear and out the other. All he could do was stare at the empty bed of the man he'd seen so many times day after day and year after year. The man he'd grown to love as though he were a brother. His best friend.

"He asked me to give you this when you woke," the nurse continued.

Tom saw her hand him a folded piece of white paper, and in a hopeless blur, he took it.

The nurse left the room, and suddenly he was alone yet again. Never in all their years together had Tom once pictured what this moment might be like. Richard, the jokester of all jokesters. His constant sarcasm and ability to make anyone crack a smile. Gone.

Tom wiped away the tears while flipping open the letter. And slowly, he brought himself to read what Richard had written.

Dear Turbo,

If you can read this chicken scratch (I took notes from our doctor on bad penmanship), then I must actually be gone. It feels odd even writing it, but for some inexplicable reason, I know it's about to happen. The pain had gone away, and then suddenly it was back. And while I was asleep, I saw my darling Marlene. Boy did I miss her, Tom.

What can I say? We've had some good times, you and I. So many years and so many breakfasts at Bertha's Diner. What's she going to do without seeing my smiling face? And what are you going to do now that you've got no one to complain with about that dumb mayor? I'm going to miss those breakfasts. And I'm going to miss you.

Looking back, I suppose I saw it coming. I saw the warning signs, but in some weird way, I always felt I was sticking around for you. When Holly died, I felt like you needed me. Someone to talk to. Someone to gripe with. But then Noel came back, and suddenly I realized you didn't need me anymore. You weren't alone anymore. You aren't alone.

I'll save all the sappy stuff for another guy, but all I can say is that I'm a better man for knowing you. I'm sorry you didn't win the Christmas Cup Competition. It's probably because they were torn between your house and mine and decided it was best to pick neither of us. Maybe you'll have better luck next year.

As my last request, I want you to stop by my house for a few things I left behind, then go home and celebrate Christmas with Noel and those kids. They need you right now, and trust me when I say you won't regret it.

Merry Christmas, my friend, Mr. Scrooge, and hopefully I'll see you again soon.

Your friend,
Richard (Putz)

Tom wiped away his tears, folded the letter, and then took one last long look at the empty bed of his friend who'd been by his side for all these years.

Outside their room, the skies had turned dark as the clock struck five. Rain continued to clamor against the window. Noel and the kids sat around the five-dollar miniature Christmas tree Noel had picked up at the grocery store the night before. In the background, the inn heater clunked into action.

After Noel had left work the day before, she'd finally gone to see Bryan, and she'd done what she knew she should have done all along. She'd let him go.

For so long, she'd focused on the wrong things because she was scared of what life might be like alone. She knew in her heart, though, that deep down, Bryan wasn't the right man for her or her kids, and as hard as it might be on her own, she had a feeling that somehow, things would work out the way they needed to.

As always, life couldn't go without hitches for Noel, and after dozens of calls to realtors, she'd discovered that none of the apartments she could afford would be available until after Christmas. But a promise was a promise, and she'd promised Tom that she'd be out by the twenty-fourth, and that wouldn't change even if he was in the hospital. So they'd packed their things and headed for the local inn for the weekend. She'd sold it to the kids as a mini-vacation and told them they could even order room service. Which, of course, they did.

They each sat holding their hot cocoas while sitting around the Christmas tree. She'd called for Tom at the hospital several times, but each time she'd tried, the nurses insisted that Tom would call her back, and each time she'd asked for an explanation, they'd offered none in return.

So it was her, Trevor, Brittany, and Evan, alone together for the first time on Christmas.

"When can we open presents, Mom?" Brittany asked.

All three kids had waited patiently all day. They'd spent most of the day watching Christmas movies and eating, with the occasional Christmas carol mixed in. Noel knew they wouldn't be as excited when they opened the presents: Trevor, with his hopes of a Playstation, and the kids, a puppy. Her budget simply didn't allow for anything like that, and she'd taken a few occasions throughout the day to remind the kids that Christmas wasn't about presents, that it was about spending time with the ones you love.

"Soon, honey. I want to see if your grandpa calls back first."

Noel gave them a soft smile, knowing their patience was wearing thin.

"Mom, are you going to see Mr. Tate for Christmas?" Brittany asked.

Noel tilted her head curiously. "I don't think so. Why do you ask, honey?"

"He was nice," Brittany returned simply.

Evan nodded his head in agreement.

"Yeah, he's a good guy, Mom," Trevor added.

Noel stared at her son for a long, hard moment. In all the years since Jacob's passing, he hadn't once talked to her about her dating in general, or even Bryan in specific, until their conversation a couple nights ago. Did the fact that he'd finally said something about a potential man in her life mean something? "Well, I'll be sure to tell him you said that."

The honest truth was that she had thought about calling him to wish him a Merry Christmas at least. Who knows what he was doing, probably spending Christmas alone. When they'd talked at the shop the day before, he hadn't mentioned anything. Clearly he was still struggling with the loss of his wife, which made complete sense. So she'd agreed that when he was ready, he'd have to be the one to ask her out. She wasn't going to be the one chasing after guys anymore. More importantly, if she did ever decide to go on a date again, she was going to take it much slower the next go-around.

Noel took another look out the window at the dark sky and view into the parking lot, with the rain beginning to slow to a steady beat. Still no call.

"Mom, can we go by Grandpa's house? You know, to see the lights?" Trevor asked.

Brittany and Evan's faces lit up at the suggestion.

"Yeah, can we, Mom?"

"Please, Mom! Maybe Grandpa's there too."

Noel looked out the window to the darkening night sky and steady rain. It did look lighter than earlier, and she supposed that seeing their Christmas lights one last time would add to the spirit of the night. But what about Tom? "Okay, okay," she finally said. "But let me try the hospital one more time before we go."

"Yay!" Brittany and Evan screamed in unison.

Trevor smiled, and they all put on their coats.

On their drive to Hidden Meadows Lane, the kids stared out the window, watching the elaborately decorated houses pass by. Still no word from Tom, but Noel supposed he was probably avoiding them on Christmas, just like he'd originally wanted to do.

They turned onto Tom's street, and soon his corner house came into view. The light show was running across the house, lighting up the front and then the side with red and green lights like a wave. Since Tom had used timers for the display this year, it meant that while he was in the hospital, the show still went on. The usual crowd of cars and people were nowhere to be found. Everyone was probably at home with the ones they love, celebrating Christ and the joys of Christmas. *It's a Wonderful Life* was playing on the garage when they rolled up next to Tom's Ford Bronco, which had been parked there since the heart attack.

"Well, shall we head inside?" Noel asked. "Maybe wait to see if Grandpa calls back?"

All three kids nodded.

Trevor, Brittany, and Evan sat at the window sill, waiting to see if anyone would come by. But aside from the occasional passing car, no one had stopped. Noel could sense their disappointment, and truthfully, she could feel it too. The magic of the crowd coming to see their house had been truly special. On top of that, without Tom around also looking through the windows, the house felt strangely empty.

Noel put on some Christmas music, started a fire in the fireplace, and then sat next to the tree as the kids continued to watch. She tried the hospital again, but still no word from Tom. Her worry was starting to grow, and now she wondered if she should just drive down there to see him anyway. What if he wasn't okay? Noel wanted to respect his wishes of not bugging him with Christmas day celebrations, but something about it just felt wrong. Something felt strangely lonely.

"Mom? Someone's walking up to the door." Brittany called.

All three kids had perked up, staring through the window. Noel got up to take a peek as well. Suddenly, the doorbell rang. She couldn't see who it was, only a silver SUV parked in front of the house.

"Who is it?" Evan asked as she backed away from the window, but Noel didn't know.

She made her way over to open the door as the kids followed secretly behind.

"Hi, Noel," a man said as the recognition hit her.

"Tate?"

Noel stared up him in his blue sweater and jeans, smiling warmly at her.

He nodded. "Hey, guys," Tate said, nodding with a wave to the kids, standing behind her.

"Hi, Mr. Tate," Brittany returned.

"What are you doing here?" Noel asked in surprise.

Tate glanced over his shoulder back toward his car, as though he were waiting for permission for something. "I think it's best if you see for yourself. Why don't you come with me?"

Tate turned to walk back down the walkway, and Noel watched, unsure of what was happening.

"Come on, Mom," Trevor said.

Noel contemplated it a second more, and then she and the kids got under the umbrella Tate held out to follow him as he walked up the sidewalk. "Where are you going?" she called.

But Tate kept on walking until he turned into Richard's sidewalk, toward the front door.

Richard's house? Had Richard made it home? They continued on behind him.

"You coming?" Tate called as he disappeared into the house.

Noel hesitated a second, closing the umbrella while the kids urged her to hurry after him.

They made their way around the corner, following Tate into the house, down the narrow entrance hallway, warm and smelling of a Christmas tree. Then the room opened up into the living room, and they saw him.

"Grandpa!" the kids called in unison, running over to give him a hug.

"Okay, okay," Tom said, his voice gravelly and soft as he wrapped his arms around them.

Noel stared down at him, sitting in a recliner beside a massive Christmas tree decorated from head to toe with lights and ornaments of all shapes, colors, and sizes. His thin face looked scruffier and more tired than she'd ever seen it, but otherwise, he seemed okay.

"What are you doing in Richard's house? And where is he?"

Tom looked over at the tree for a long moment before reaching for something hanging from one of the branches, then he glanced up to meet Noel's gaze. "Richard asked me to stop by his house, so I could give you this."

All eyes focused on Noel when he reached out to hand her an envelope.

Confused, Noel grabbed it, blinking back at Tom. She studied the envelope for a moment before turning it over and peeling it open.

Dear Noel,

Boy, how nice it's been seeing the wonderful, beautiful woman you've grown into over the years. Not without hardships, but you've certainly become a stronger person because of it.

For years, I've put up with your father. You and I both know how hard that is to do. But along the way, we've grown as close as brothers. Although he can be difficult, he's one of the best men I've ever met. He's got a good heart in him, figuratively of course.

The reason I am writing you is because he and I both need your help. He won't admit it, but I will for him. Since Holly's passing, he's taken her loss out on himself. And because of that, he pushed everyone away. As someone who knows him as well as I do, I can assure you, it was only with the best of intentions. He didn't want to see you hurt.

Please take care of him for me. He needs you.

As you may have guessed in receiving this letter, my time is up. And I must say, it's been a pleasure.

Her breathing stopped. Did it mean what she thought it did? She looked over to Tom.

Tom nodded, his expression solemn.

She felt the pit in her stomach drop just a bit, a small part of her missing. Her neighbor and Tom's best friend for all the years she'd been alive. The funny, lively, skinny, scrappy man who always knew exactly what to say to put a smile on her face. She wiped away a tear and looked back down to the letter, her heart throbbing in her chest.

Marlene and I always wanted kids but never saw that wish come true. As such, I've got no one to pass my things down to, and because of that, I truly hope you will accept them. My lawyer has the official will, but the first of which is my house.

I know it might get difficult living next door to Tom, and I would understand if you'd prefer simply selling it in order to find another place. I am also leaving Tom with one hundred thousand dollars that he doesn't know about yet, and I need your help to make sure he spends it. Medical bills aren't cheap, but he also needs to do something with the termite damage and that dang lawn. The neighbors have started to complain and I can't keep making excuses for him any longer. Needless to say, you'll see the check soon.

Second, I know this isn't an easy responsibility to bear, but Christie has truly enjoyed the company of your kids. If you want her, I'm sure she'd love to be a part of your family. If not, then Tom's getting the short end of the stick.

Last, there are a few presents under the tree I instructed my lawyer to pick up. I hope they help make your Christmas special. Thanks for the memories, Noel, and Merry Christmas.

Your neighbor,
Richard Sampson

A tear streamed down Noel's face as she looked up from the letter, an overwhelming flurry of emotions rushing in.

As always, he'd used humor in his last letter and words to her, and he'd ended it on a high note. A high note Noel couldn't truly fathom. Richard had left them his house. The house Richard and Marlene had built their life in. And he'd left money to take care of his best friend as well. What a beautiful, unbelievable thing.

"I think we might have a little something in the other room for the kids, if it's okay with Noel," Tom stated.

Noel looked up knowingly and nodded. Having a dog wouldn't be easy, but what in life was?

"Tate, would you mind?" Tom asked.

"Not at all," Tate said.

He disappeared into the other room while the kids waited anxiously for what it might be, then he re-emerged with a partner to accompany him. A big red bow sat atop Christie's fluffy white head. Her tongue was hanging out of the side of her mouth, and her tail started wagging furiously from side to side.

"Christie!" Evan yelled as he and Brittany jumped up.

"How come Christie has a bow?" Brittany asked.

Christie leapt into Brittany's arms and began to lick her face, and then she squirmed into Evan's arms and began licking him too.

"Well, you said you wanted a dog, right?" Noel said.

"Wait, are you saying we can keep Christie?" Brittany asked, she and Evan's eyes brimming with anticipation.

"What about Richard?" Trevor asked.

Noel took a deep breath, wiping away a tear. "Richard is back with his wife. He needs someone to look after Christie while he's gone. And yes, if you promise to walk her and feed her and watch after her every day, then you can keep her."

Trevor let out a sad, knowing sigh. He understood what had happened to Richard.

Evan and Brittany jumped in excitement, oblivious to what Noel had meant, and began to play with their new dog.

"Trevor, I think Richard left you something under the tree. Why don't you open it?" Tom asked.

Trevor looked down at the boxes, a sad look across his face. He searched until he found a big red one with his name on it.

"Go on," Tom said.

Trevor lifted it onto his lap and then began to peel it open. Within a second of opening it, his face went from solemn to shocked. He peeled back the paper some more until a brand new Playstation revealed itself. "Is this real?" Trevor asked.

"Yup. Richard wanted to make sure you got it after what you did to help him outside with the house. He really appreciated your hard work," Tom said on Richard's behalf.

Trevor broke into a sheepish grin. "I'm going to miss him, and I'm never going to forget that sunset with you and him, sitting on his lawn drinking Coke."

Tom nodded in agreement.

"Noel, do you mind if we speak a moment?" Tate asked.

Noel looked over to him and nodded.

Tate led her through the hallway and then outside onto the front porch. The chilly night air brushed over her face while the sprinkles continued to fall.

"I'm guessing my father asked you to drive him home from the hospital?" Noel started. She had a feeling that Tom had had something up his sleeve. Otherwise he could have simply asked her to pick him up.

"Yup. And I was happy to help," Tate replied.

"Really nice of you."

"Thanks." Tate paused for a moment, and then he asked, "So, I take it you decided not to get back with your ex?"

"You would be right. As easy as it would be financially, getting back with him just wasn't right. He wasn't the one, as much as I wanted him to be."

Tate nodded. "I'm glad."

Noel felt a wave of little butterflies in her stomach. "You are, are you?"

"I like you, Noel." Tate reached over to touch her arm, which sent her heart fluttering even faster.

Noel smiled up at him. "I like you too, Tate."

"I know I said it before, but it's just hard. I haven't dated anyone since Alice passed, and truthfully, I don't know if I'm even ready yet, but I know that I feel something between us. And as corny as it might sound, I feel like I ended up moving a thousand miles away for a reason, and I believe you came by the coffee shop looking for a job for that same reason. Who knows, maybe that reason will only last a short bit, but what I do know is that I'm willing to find out."

Noel's heart raced and her nerves tingled as she tried to contain her grin. It'd been a long time since a man had truly made her blush and get nervous, and for the first time in a long time, it finally felt right. "Me too. I think we just take it one step at a time. I rushed into my last relationship, and don't want to do that again. All I know is that I like you and your beard and your jokes and your generosity, and that I want to know you better." She stared into his eyes for a long hard moment until her gaze began flickering between his eyes and lips.

"Mom?" Brittany called.

Noel and Tate broke into an awkward laugh as they looked through the door back down the hall.

"Better get over there," Tate said.

Noel and the kids opened the presents Richard had left, each laughing as Christie jumped from person to person, licking them as she did. They shared laughs and smiles around the Christmas tree, simply enjoying each other's company.

Richard had given Brittany ballet slippers, and Evan a basketball and a tub of army men. Trevor had the Playstation, and Noel a waffle maker. She had a feeling it had something to do with Tom and Richard's Tuesdays at Bertha's Diner, which surely wouldn't be the same anymore. Richard left Tom a hose, which they all had a good laugh at because of the fact that his lawn was so dead and ugly.

Soon, they made their way back over to Tom's house, Christie and all, where they noticed a car parked out front and a man standing at their door. Noel peered in through the car windows, trying to make out who was inside.

The man turned toward them and smiled. "Mr. VanHansen. It's Alex. Alex Garcetti."

Noel squinted as the familiar face of the man who'd won the Christmas Cup Competition for the sixth time in a row came slowly into view.

Tom shook the man's hand as Noel, Tate, and the kids waited behind.

"I don't want to take much of your time, but my family really thought you should have this." Alex handed Tom a crisp golden envelope.

Tom looked down at it, and Noel leaned in as Tom ran a finger along the seam. Inside was a Christmas card, silver and white with snow and sparkles splashed across it. Tom opened it and suddenly a thin slip of paper slid out. He grabbed it before it hit the wet ground, then they each read the inside.

From our family to yours, Merry Christmas. We hope this makes the holidays a little bit brighter.
    From the Garcettis.

Tom held up the thin slip of paper and then flipped it over. His jaw dropped open and Noel's eyes went wide.

"What is it, Mom?" Brittany asked while Evan jumped up to sneak a glance.

Noel knew exactly what it was, but it took a moment for her brain to fully process what it meant. She stared at Tom in disbelief. In his hands was a check for $16,812.

Tom finally looked up. "I can't accept this. Please," he said, handing it back to Alex.

Alex shook his head. "It's not mine to take back. This was actually my wife's idea. And I'm not going to be the one to go against what she wants. Trust me, she wants you to have it. You guys have a heck of a Christmas display, and truthfully, you should have been the ones to win."

Noel looked past Alex to his wife and their daughters, standing under an umbrella at the side of the house, smiling softly at Noel and the kids.

Alex turned to walk back out along the walkway, and then he slid a hand around Samantha's waist. Samantha gave Tom a slow, reassuring nod.

Tom and Noel simply stared at them in shock. Samantha had been the one to insist on giving Tom the winnings? The Samantha who'd bullied her and had made a point of announcing her own lighting ceremony at Tom's house? Noel suddenly realized that the woman she thought she knew maybe wasn't so bad after all. Maybe all she really wanted was to be accepted, and the best way she'd known to do that was by making sure the attention was on her. But here she was now, with no audience to flaunt her gesture, choosing to give $16,000 to Tom, and for that, Noel felt extremely grateful.

Samantha and Alex disappeared toward the side of the house.

A second later, Kayla ran up the entryway straight to Trevor. In one swift movement, she leaned in and kissed him square on the cheek. Trevor went a brighter red than Noel had ever seen before.

"Merry Christmas, Trevor," she said, laughing as she grabbed Trevor's hand. She skipped off down the sidewalk to join her family on the side of the house with Trevor in tow.

"I wouldn't mind watching *It's a Wonderful Life*. Shall we join them?" Tate asked.

Noel looked up into his deep brown eyes and then nodded. With that, Tate held up the umbrella for Noel as Tom followed behind with a cane in one hand and his umbrella in the other for Evan and Brittany.

Alex, Samantha, their other daughter, Kayla, and Trevor, as well as several other families, gathered around the garage at the side of the house to watch *It's a Wonderful Life* together.

Noel, Tate, Brittany, Evan, and Tom joined the group.

Tom walked over to shake Alex's hand, and Noel made her way over to Samantha.

"You guys really put on a great display," Samantha said.

"And so did you." They each turned to watch the movie; the part where George realizes that his life wasn't so bad after all and runs back to the bridge to beg for his life back. "Samantha, that was a really nice thing you did. I don't know what I can ever do to repay you."

Samantha turned her head to lock Noel's gaze. "Look, I know I've been wrong in the past, but just know I'm trying to be better. Please don't worry about the money; it's yours and you all deserve it."

Noel contemplated saying something else, but then she realized that Samantha had said it all. Samantha was changing too, just like they all were. And with those changes came a generosity Noel couldn't have ever expected.

"Thank you, Samantha."

They both smiled.

A few moments later, Noel went back to join Tate under the umbrella, while Tom turned to them after he finished thanking Alex.

"Well, what are the chances of that?" Tom said while staring up.

"Of what, Dad?" Noel asked.

"I put up one more decoration in honor of your mother before going to the hospital that morning of the ceremony, and it looks like you two just so happened to be standing right under it."

Noel looked up into the tree to see what her father was talking about, when suddenly it all made sense. The story of Tom and Holly and their annual dates at the Christmas Festival, always capped off by a kiss under the mistletoe that wasn't mistletoe—holly. Now, of all places, and all nights, she just so happened to be standing under her very own holly with Tate by her side.

Their eyes met as Tate smiled that same warm, welcoming smile he had the first day Noel had met him. All at once, she felt herself moving toward him as he moved in. A warm burst of energy shot down her spine as his lips met hers and his body moved in closer, warming her against the cold night air. It was just him and her, and for that moment, nothing else mattered. Their eyes stayed on each other for a long while after they slowly pulled away, until finally they realized they weren't alone.

Tom laughed aloud as Tate slipped his arm behind her back and they each turned to watch the ending of the movie. Brittany and Evan petted Christie, while Trevor and Kayla stood hand in hand beside each other. Everyone watched together under their umbrellas with the drizzling rain falling all around.

Noel knew that the kiss hadn't been just any kiss. No, she hadn't felt something like that since she'd first met Jacob. It was undeniable that something had happened between her and Tate. The spark had finally ignited. But she'd also felt a presence overhead, like someone watching over her.

Maybe it was Jacob, maybe it was Holly, maybe it was Alice, or maybe it was Richard. All she knew was that whoever it was, they were happy. And for the first time in a long time, she was too.

Tom stepped back to stand beside her. Brittany and Evan followed with Christie behind as he leaned in to whisper three simple words she hadn't heard from him in two years, "Merry Christmas, Noel."

Noel felt a tear fall down her cheek as Tom slid his arm around her shoulder, with Tate standing on her other side. Images of her father twenty years younger, the man she'd missed for so long, played through her head. Images of her, Tom, and Holly standing arm-in-arm beside the Christmas tree, singing Christmas carols together. She smiled as they cast their gazes forward to watch the movie. "Merry Christmas, Dad."

ACKNOWLEDGMENTS

This story had a lot of great people to help it get it here. First, I want to thank the team at Cedar Fort for believing in the book and also for all the phenomenal effort it took to push it across the finish line. Briana for believing in it initially; Markie for an amazing cover; Kaitlin, Jessilyn, and Deborah for the beautiful interior and edits. Thank you also to my early editor, Amanda. I know editing a Christmas book in summer isn't the easiest of tasks.

This story is a personal one for me, the inspiration for it being a year from my youth. What could and should have been a difficult and sad Christmas ended up being the most magical and memorable one yet. I want to thank my family for putting in so much effort to make Christmas special for us in such difficult times: my mother, grandmothers, grandfathers, father, brother, sister, and aunt. Next, I want to thank someone who I hadn't met yet during the time this story took place, but who pushes me to be the best person I can be, and who supports me in all my crazy endeavors: my wife. I'm reminded every day of how lucky I am to have you.

Last, thank you to you, the reader. I hope this story can help to inspire or at least spread a little Christmas cheer. Christmas can be a difficult time for some, but it can also be a great time to simply focus on the people that mean the most to us. And sometimes, that's all we need. Thank you so much for reading, and Merry Christmas.

About the Author

Trenton Hughes self-published his first Christmas book, *The Christmas Note*, with the intention of only giving it out to his family. But shortly after the release in November 2012, the book gained unexpected traction and quickly became a Christmas hit. He graduated with a bachelor's in high technology business from San Jose State University, then pursued a career as a content writer while writing his second book, *Counting on Christmas*, on the side. He now resides in sunny Southern California. For updates and more information, visit TrentonHughes.com.